CW00606563

THE CUCKOO'S DAUGHTER

When Louisa is called "The Cuckoo's Daughter" by a fairground gypsy, she is surprised and angry. Now sixteen, she has lived all her life on a farm with her foster-parents and family but they refuse to tell her the names of her real parents. She longs to find out who they were. Discovering a hidden miniature portrait, she wonders if it is of her mother, but she still meets a wall of secrecy.

She falls in love with handsome Godfrey Macdonald but her foster-father refuses to allow them to marry and sends her to a horrible boarding-school.

Will she be brave enough to escape the school and elope with Godfrey, leaving the only family she knows and the foster-sister she loves? And will she find out the truth about her real parents?

"You have used your material most skilfully and the story is very well told. I am enjoying every page..."
SIR MICHAEL HOLROYD

THE
CUCKOO'S DAUGHTER

BY
GRISELDA GIFFORD

To Dousy

with best wish

Griselda Gifford

COUNTRY BOOKS

Published by Country Books/Ashridge Press
Courtyard Cottage, Little Longstone, Bakewell, Derbyshire DE45 1NN
Tel: 01629 640670
e-mail: dickrichardson@country-books.co.uk
www.countrybooks.biz

ISBN 978-1-906789-87-9

Printed and bound in England by:
4edge Ltd. Hockley, Essex

DEDICATION

*With much love to my husband, Jim,
and thanks to my children,
Mark and Niki, for their support.*

ACKNOWLEDGEMENTS

This is based on a true story but many of the incidents and characters are of my own invention. I am Louisa Macdonald's great-great grand-daughter and I felt her story had to be told, as she was so badly treated by her real parents.

Some of the characters are real: The Rev. Wadham Diggle was a Rector in the Esher area. The disgusting "Priest", Joseph Paisley, did perform weddings at that time at Gretna Green but I don't know which doubtful clergy Louisa and Godfrey chose. The Tyrconnells were a real family and you can visit the National Trust gardens at Claremont – the house is now a school.

I would like to acknowledge help from:

Lord Macdonald
The Macdonald Centre at Armadale, Skye
Sir Ian Macdonald
"Family Tapestry" by Averil Stewart
Hull University Records Office
Dr. Lucy Worsley
The Story of Esher by Ian D.Stevens
Mrs. Patricia Flippance, for historical details and dress.
Kiplin Hall
Claremont Fan Court School
My husband, Dr J E Hall
My children, Mark and Niki Gifford
Margaret Nash and Stephanie Baudet, fellow authors.
Dick Richardson of Country Books

CHAPTER 1

1799. ESHER, SURREY

"Missed it!"

I laughed as my sister Bet leaped wildly in the air, trying to hit the shuttlecock with her bat. It sailed over the hedge into the road just as we heard the clopping of hooves coming down the lane. I heard the rider dismount and the shuttlecock was thrown back.

"Here you are, ladies!"

I caught a brief glimpse of a handsome young man, wearing a soldier's red uniform. "Thank you, sir," I called back.

His large blue eyes seemed to look straight into mine as he smiled widely, lifted his hat and trotted off.

Bet giggled. "Lou! You're blushing! He was certainly a fine gentleman and an officer. I saw those gold bits on his shoulders."

I felt a strange shiver of excitement and I couldn't help wondering if I'd ever see that blue-eyed officer again. "I expect he's one of the soldiers we've seen coming back from the war in the Lowlands."

"Probably," Bet said. "A tattered looking lot, marching through the village from their ship at Portsmouth. I heard Pa say they lost that battle." She picked up the bats and shuttle-cock and grabbed my arm. "Come on, Lou. You know we said we'd help at the dairy now Marigold's away ill." She began to run up the field towards the farm.

I liked living at the farm but I'd much rather have stayed outside on this sparkling September morning. Still, my foster-mother was hard-pressed when one of the dairy-maids was away sick and I wanted to help.

"Coming!" I picked up my skirts and ran after her.

"It's the Michaelmas Fair tomorrow," Bet said when I caught up with her. "You'll be passing the Green when Dick collects you from your lessons at the Rectory. I wager I'll be sent to do something boring like cleaning out the hen-house or fetching flour from the Mill."

"Bet, you're only just fourteen." I tried to ignore my foster-sister's scowl. "Too young to go to the Fair alone. Dick will be in a hurry to get back to his work at Claremont so I won't stay long."

He was my favourite foster-brother in the big Edsir family, the family I had known from babyhood but could never really call my own.

Bet ran ahead again, shouting back, "Too young, too young! Everyone says that but I'm not too young to help on the farm. Come on, Lou – we've work to do. Stop dreaming about the Fair."

When we reached the dairy with its familiar smell of milk and the sound of the cows lowing in the barn, I smiled at Bet. "If you stop sulking I'll buy you something from the Fair."

"There's always a fortune-teller. I'll wager you'll spend all your money on her," Bet said but she was smiling again. She never stayed angry for long.

If Dick let me, I probably would see the fortune-teller. But I wanted to know my past, as well as my future. Sometimes I was wholly happy at the farm but at other times, I felt a kind of loneliness and wished with all my heart I knew my parents. This feeling had grown lately and I was beginning to resent the secrecy surrounding my birth.

It was time to find out the truth.

CHAPTER 2

"You have a lucky face," the old gypsy droned.

I almost giggled, as this was what every gypsy who came to the door, selling white heather or bits of lace, had assured me.

"If you follow your heart you will pain those close to you. I see many children."

I again tried not to laugh. The gypsy caravan was hot and the old woman reeked of onions and fusty layers of clothes. "I hope you can see marriage if I'm to have all those children!"

Her dark eyes were suddenly menacing. "Yes – but you will have to be…" She fumbled her words and said something in the Gypsy tongue. When she realised I didn't understand she went on, "You'll be needing strength and courage to go with your love."

"And what's he like, this future husband?" I asked.

"Cross my palm with silver," the old woman muttered.

I nearly refused but there was something hypnotic about those eyes. Dick, who was waiting impatiently outside, would laugh and say I was wasting money. "I have no silver but these coins." I put them in the gypsy's claw-like hand.

"He's very tall and strong and rides a fine horse. Blue eyes, ruddy cheeks…"

That could be Dick, or anybody, for that matter.

"His name?" I asked impatiently but she thrust her hand forward again.

I shook my head and the gypsy's face closed up, her mouth a slit between her big nose and bony chin. I got up to go but the old woman grabbed my arm so hard it hurt.

Her voice was loud now. "Your mother was like the cuckoo, leaving you in a stranger's nest. You are the cuckoo's daughter!" She sniggered as if it pleased her.

All the dizzy happiness of the day vanished. "What rubbish!" I said loudly. "And anyway, the cuckoo's fledgling kills its brothers and sisters so it can get all the food. I love my family."

The old woman's laughter followed me as I stumbled down the caravan steps, feeling strangely shaken and angry. Had my mother dumped me, like the cuckoo – or did she really die, as I'd been told?

Dick must have heard the old woman's last loud words and he frowned as he hurried me away. "Lou – you've been an age hearing that rubbish and wasting your money. I'm sure I saw our Bet earlier but she ran off. She'll tell them where you are."

"She'll be in trouble, going to the fair on her own," I said. "I don't think she'll tell." But I knew Bet's moods could change in a trice. "I've bought her marchpane to eat – that should sweeten her. Didn't you want to bowl for the pig?"

He nodded and guided me across the Green and through the throng of villagers at the Michaelmas Fair stalls, selling vegetables, lace, sweetmeats, ribbons, herbs, small beer and mead. For the first time, I noticed some of the girls looking at my tall brother. His fair hair was bleached by the sun and his sun-tanned bare arms and shoulders rippled with muscle. It was as if I'd never looked at him properly before and it was a strange feeling.

Dick glanced at the church clock. "We must be quick. I have to get back to the stables at Claremont or Carter will be after me. I said I would stay on and clean the harness tonight to make up the time. And all for you, my dear sister." His smile was affectionate.

The pig was small and pink, squealing as it tried to look through the bars of its cage. I was sorry for the poor little creature. I ought to be used to farming ways but I was always sad to see animals being penned up, then sent for slaughter. I'd been teased when I was younger, and refused to eat the Christmas goose, who for months before ran to me for food and let me stroke his soft feathers.

The ninepins were at some yards distant, arranged cunningly so it was hard to knock them all over.

Dick bowled three times but still a ninepin remained.

"I want to try," I said.

Both men stared at me as I seized the hard wooden ball and threw it wildly, with all my strength, knocking all the ninepins over.

The old man grumbled but agreed I'd won. "But I be warning you, that creature's the runt of the litter and may never make bacon."

I already loved the piglet, wriggling in Dick's arms. "She'll never be bacon!" I felt sick at the thought. "I shall call her Bertha."

As we walked away, Dick said, "You know, Pa isn't going to be pleased. Not unless you'll fatten the pig for Christmas."

Something inside me was rebelling and I refused to think of the row brewing ahead. "I shall look after her," I said firmly, taking the piglet from him. The creature grunted and felt warm in my arms, even if she did smell rather piggy.

We were on the road near the farm when I felt the trickle of urine from the piglet and at that moment, the Tyrconnells' coach came along, drawn by perfectly matched dark bay horses. The Countess was staring very hard at us but her daughter, Lady Susan, was smiling.

Dick laughed. "They'll not be bringing you any more presents now! And I'm sick of wondering why they come to a dairy farm to see you. Our Bet gets real jealous. I reckon they employed your mother and knew who your father was." He stopped but I knew what he meant – that my mother, perhaps a servant, had been seduced by one of that aristocratic

13

household. I felt a shiver of dislike at the thought.

The piglet nuzzled its damp snout into my neck as if to apologise for wetting me.

"I don't know why the Tyrconnells come to see me. Nobody will tell me but I mean to find out," I said quietly. "Mama Edsir's told me some story about my mother dying and my father a soldier who may have been killed abroad, but I'm not sure I believe it now I'm older."

"Why bother? You're happy with us, aren't you?" he asked as they walked back to the farm.

The piglet was wriggling again making me stumble on the deeply rutted road, Dick put his arm round me. It didn't feel brotherly any more.

"Why do we have to grow up?" I asked suddenly. "Remember how we used to slide down straw-stacks with Bet and play those games of hide and seek?"

"I remember. And the times you rode bareback on the pony, sliding down his neck when he stopped suddenly! But everyone has to grow up, Lou."

I couldn't tell him I didn't want our relationship to change so I said, "All the fuss of not going out on my own just because I'm a girl. No point in growing up if you can't get away sometimes."

"They want you to become a young lady – Miss Louisa La Coast."

Now he was teasing me. "I've always hated that name," I muttered. "And I'm not sure I want to be a young lady. I've never been further than the market at Darking. I'd like to see London town or even the wilds of Scotland or Wales."

"You'll be saying next you want to go to Australia with the convicts." Dick laughed. "I'm happy to stay in Esher and learn to drive the Tyrconnells' coach – then marry a pretty girl." His arm tightened round me. "And bring up a clutch of young 'uns."

I shifted sideways, out of his grip.

We were nearing the farm now. "I'll come with you to see Pa," he said. "He'll not be best pleased unless we can say the piglet will be fattened for market. Maybe she could be kept for breeding."

"I'm not scared of him."

Then I thought that wasn't entirely true. Farley Edsir had a quick temper and he could bellow like a bull, if he was crossed. But I was tired of being Good Little Louisa. It was time to summon up my courage and say what I felt.

"He's softer with you than with us," Dick said. "All us boys got beaten regular and the girls got a slap. Sometimes I think it's because he's sorry for you – not knowing your parents or is someone paying him for his silence?"

I didn't answer but walked a little way ahead, thinking it out. Could he be right? It sounded underhand – unpleasant, even. Maybe it was better to stick to the tale I'd been told.

As we neared home, my young foster-brother, Tom, came running. "You're in big trouble, Lou," he panted. "Those snooty Tyrconnells paid us a surprise visit and our Bet told them where you'd gone. A right tell-tale, she is." He looked at the pig and giggled. "Pissed on you, has it? Serves you right. I wanted to go to the Michaelmas Fair but Pa made me clean out the byre."

Dick frowned at his younger brother. "You know well that was because of what you did in church last Sunday."

Tom looked down at his dirty boots and I saw there were feathers in his straw-coloured mop of hair.

I wanted to giggle, thinking of last Sunday, when the Rector's long and very boring sermon, oft repeated, was interrupted by scuffling and giggles amongst the choir-boys. Tom, crimson-faced was reaching up to the Tyrconnells' private pew, to capture his tame field-mouse.

He laughed now. "It was worth it, seeing her Ladyship leap up like that and all them feathers in her hat a-quiver, like it was going to fly off."

15

"At least Lady Susan caught the mouse for you," I said. "Some girls wouldn't have touched it."

Dick frowned. "She's a pretty girl but I've heard things about her mother."

"What things?"

"You're too young for such gossip, Lou," was his irritating answer.

Now we were near the oak-beamed farmhouse, which fitted snugly into the sheltering trees. "Dick – you'd best get back to the stables," I said. "It will take you nearly an hour as it is." I knew how much his job as stable-boy at Claremont meant to him, as a step to his ambition to be coachman. I looked at Tom. "You'll help me find a pen for the piglet, won't you?"

He nodded.

He was my favourite brother, after Dick, and I remembered mothering him when I was four or so, rocking his wooden cradle and picking him up if he cried. Now he was always ready to help me.

Dick touched my arm lightly. "I'll go. Blame the whole thing on me, Lou. Say I persuaded you to go to the Fair." He ran off with an easy loping stride.

It was too late to hide the piglet. Farley Edsir was coming out of the farmhouse, waving his stick, with his wife hanging on his other arm, trying to pull him back. My darling young spaniel, Tobias, rushed up to me, muddying my skirt as he stood on his hind legs to see the piglet.

"Louisa – where have you been, Miss?" Papa Edsir bellowed, as loudly as if he were shouting at his prize bull. "And what are you doing with that there runt of a piglet?"

Mary Edsir detached herself and hurried to my side, as if to defend me. "Oh dear, just look at you! The little pig has…" she stopped delicately.

"…piddled on her clothes." Her husband believed in calling a spade a spade. "Her ladyship and Lady Susan called just

16

now to see you and Bet told them you was at the Fair with Dick. I'd sent her to see why you was so long coming back from the Rectory."

"Her Ladyship was upset, dear." Mary Edsir looked worried, as she often did. "After all, they bring you all those presents – you have to be grateful."

"Why?" I asked softly. I agreed with Bet, for once, that it was unfair to single me out.

The piglet was tickling my neck so I found it hard not to giggle. "Dick and I had to cross the Green and I wanted to spend a little time at the Fair," I said. "After all, you let us all go last year, Papa."

He looked as if he might explode. "Answering back now, are we? Miss Louisa La Coast – you will never marry if you behave like this." He turned to Tom. "Take that piglet away now. I suppose she might fatten up for Christmas."

I couldn't help crying out, "No!" but Mr. Edsir took no notice as he almost pushed me into the stone-flagged hall. Bet was peeking round a door, perhaps feeling guilty for telling tales.

Mama Edsir clutched at his arm. "Farley – remember who she is. She is a special daughter, our gift." Her voice was soft.

"I don't like being called Louisa La Coast," I said quietly. My heart was thudding but I was going to defy him for once. "It's a silly, made-up name, only fit for an actress. Why can't you tell me who my real parents were and why the Tyrconnells bring me presents and yet refuse to tell me why they come."

Mr Edsir's face was purple now as he shouted, "I have told you, Louisa – your mother died in childbirth and your father was in the Army, possibly killed in America. And I'll thank you to remember you are a young lady of sixteen now, and behave like one. Her ladyship wants you to share a Governess with Lady Susan, as you are about the same age. Of course, I agreed. Such an honour and an opportunity for you."

"A very generous offer," Mary Edsir chimed in with a

17

nervous smile. "And they have been so kind, giving Dick his job in the stables. I know the Tyrconnells want you to become a Young Lady. That was why they wanted you to go to the Rectory, to play the harpsichord and learn from the Reverend's books than I could teach you – also to improve your sewing with the Reverend Diggle's sister."

I thought of Miss Dorothy Diggle, frowning at my knotted sampler but I'd enjoyed the music and the pleasure of dipping into the Rector's library.

I pushed my untidy curls out of my face, conscious of my damp and smelly clothes. I felt uncomfortable as well as indignant – I hated being ordered around like a wayward pet who had to lick the smart boots of the Tyrconnells, just because they were rich and titled.

But I had to admit I was tempted by the thought of seeing inside the grand mansion at Claremont where there would certainly be a harpsichord and beautiful grounds where I could sketch. And Lady Susan might own those forbidden Romances, not found at the Rectory nor at the farm, where Mr. Edsir only approved of the Bible or the works of William Shakespeare.

Bet had sneaked on me just now but she was jealous and I couldn't blame her.

"I'll go if Bet can come too." I stared defiantly at my foster-father.

"Bargaining now, are we?" He'd explode any minute! "You will go where you are told, Louisa Maria. You will never marry well if you behave like this. Remember, you have no money of your own, no dowry to offer a suitor. It's my duty to make you behave like a gentlewoman. Go to your room at once and stay there until you see fit to apologise. You shall miss your dinner."

I turned and ran up the stairs, almost crying with anger and sadness. So was that what the Edsirs had felt all my life – they were just doing their duty, bringing me up?

18

I was glad when Tobias followed me – I felt so lonely. He trotted after me as I paced up and down the wooden boards of my room, so sloping that small objects slid down in the night, moving as if by ghostly power.

I heard a clattering below as old Annie roused herself to serve the dinner and there was a smell of rabbit stew wafting up, together with the yeasty smell of new bread. Breakfast had been early but I tried to ignore my hunger.

Tobias leaped onto the elaborate bed-cover. That was another annoying thing – as well as my foster-parents insisting on moving me out of the room I shared with Bet, the Tyrconnells had sent me this beautifully embroidered bed-cover, while Bet just had a patchwork quilt on her bed. I'd protested but, as usual, I'd had been told how ungrateful I was.

"They think we treat you like Cinderella," Bet had said bitterly. "Now they are your Fairy Godmothers you'll be going to the Ball and finding a handsome Prince."

I'd laughed. "You're pretty, not a bit like an Ugly Sister."

One of the other presents from the Tyrconnells had been a looking-glass for my room. I stared at it now and saw my crumpled dress, my tumbled red hair, and those freckles on my nose which I didn't like. At least my waist was small, especially in the hated stays. In my new rage of defiance, I took everything off, and sat on the bed in my shift next to Tobias. I didn't care that he was muddying the cover with dirty paws.

I was annoyed to find I was crying, angry tears, as I felt rejected even by my foster-family. And why wouldn't Mary Edsir tell me where my mother was buried? She always said she didn't know – that the carriage had come by night, with a wet-nurse carrying me, a day-old baby.

Tobias licked my face and I hugged him close. He was the one present from the Tyrconnells I really valued, even if he got into trouble. I almost smiled as I thought of his stealing a leg of lamb from the meat-safe last week. The Edsirs were out and Bet helped me catch the dog, wrest the leg from him and cover the bite-marks with rosemary and bacon fat.

Tobias leaped off the bed at the sound of hooves on the cobbled yard below. I followed him, looking through the small window overlooking the stable-yard and the farm buildings. A smart black horse was clattering into the yard, ridden by a groom wearing the Duke's livery. Every so often a messenger would summon Mr. Edsir to Hampton Court, a few miles away, where he acted as the Duke of Gloucester's steward.

I waited and was pleased to see Farley Edsir hurry from the house, mounting his big roan cob and riding off with the messenger. The old house seemed to sigh and creak with relief, emptied of Farley's booming voice and bossy ways.

Then I saw Tom, bringing our pony Billy and the dog-cart out of the shed and Mama heaving her plump body inside. She must be taking the opportunity of visiting her friend, Bessie Carter. I guessed she would boast that her foster-daughter was going to be taught by a proper Governess at Claremont. I felt a bit sick, thinking of going there. Would they laugh at my country ways? Lady Susan was only a little older than me. Would she look down her nose at me? I told myself that the new Louisa was going to be strong – and even more determined to find out the secret of her birth.

It was then I had an idea – but Bet was still here and this was something I had to do on my own. I was just turning away from the window when I heard a loud whistling and I saw Cal, the pedlar, was coming to the back door. In a moment, Bet was out there, always drawn by Callum's sweet Irish voice and his tray of everything from ribbons to love-potions. I knew how long they would chatter, Cal almost flirting with my young sister.

I'd risk it. I tied a lead to Tobias' collar and went out into the dark corridor.

It was strange that I'd never thought before that there might be a clue to my birth, hidden somewhere in the house. At the back of my mind, I had thought the Edsirs would tell me the whole story when I was grown but now I didn't think this would ever happen.

There was a smell of wood-smoke, candles and the bread, rising by the kitchen fire, where old Annie snoozed in her chair. Where would precious things be hidden? I'd try upstairs first and if I drew a blank, downstairs on another day.

My heart thudding, I went past the door to the room I'd shared with Bet, past Dick and Tom's room and the two empty rooms, once slept in by the four elder Edsirs before they left to be married. I hesitated outside Mary and Farley Edsir's bedroom, trying to convince myself that nothing would be hidden there.

Then I remembered boring hours with Bet upstairs in the sewing-room on the top floor, hemming and mending the linen and darning a pile of socks. I'd seen a small chest. Mary Edsir told us it held clothes and mementos dear to her, like her wedding dress.

I tugged Tobias up the steep little flight of stairs and went into the sewing-room, pushing past a table laden with boxes of threads and needles to where the box sat on the window-ledge. Would it be locked?

I felt guilty and my fingers fumbled at the lid, which opened easily. There was a strong smell of rosemary and lavender. On top was a bundle wrapped in plain cloth. I unwrapped it carefully and found an elaborate rose silk dress. This must be Mama Edsir's wedding-dress.

Then I looked underneath, finding two more silk dresses, of the fashion not worn now and not needed by a farmer's wife. I pounced on a packet, tied with a pink ribbon but they were Christening certificates for the eight Edsir children but not for me.

Tobias whined and I heard Bet's distant voice, in the kitchen far below. I'd have to hurry.

I was going to give up when I saw a big embroidered bag

with a draw-thread top. Feeling like a thief, I took it out. It was full of baby clothes, edged with fine lace and underneath, a tiny pair of white kid shoes, almost doll-sized and a cob-web-thin lace shawl. Had the Edsir children been christened in these clothes? They were beautifully sewn and made of fine soft muslin. The Edsirs weren't rich and the lace was exquisite. Could they have been my baby clothes?

Under the clothes I found a white velvet pouch.

Inside was a miniature of a beautiful woman and a note, written on thick cream vellum. Just a few words: "*Take care of Louisa Maria.*"

I could hear my heart-beat thudding in my ears and I wanted to cry. My mother must have written this on her death-bed. So she *had* cared about her baby.

The miniature painting must be of my mother. Nobody in the Edsir family could have afforded such a thing. I stared at my lovely mother. She was looking slightly to one side, with a wistful expression in her large blue eyes and she held a dove in her arms. I knew this was a symbol of peace and purity. Was this painted before she met my father? Did he treat her well? Perhaps he left her penniless, rejected by her family, so she couldn't keep her baby. Yes, that was it. I kissed the miniature and knew I had to keep it.

The next moment there was a clattering on the attic stairs and Bet burst in. "What are you doing, Lou? What's that in your hand? Let's see."

I showed her. "I've found a painting of my mother and I mean to keep it."

"She's beautiful," Bet said. "I wonder why it was hidden away. And how do you know she's your mother?" She looked again. "I suppose she does look a little like you."

I showed her the note. "So she did care, after all! I expect she was dying when she wrote it."

Bet's brown eyes glistened with easy tears. "That's so sad, Lou."

"Promise you won't tell?"

"I won't but Mama will find it's gone, although she'd not believe that her goody-goody Louisa would steal anything, unlike me, raiding the larder for cakes." Bet giggled.

"If she finds out I'll tell her it's mine and she had no right to hide it from me."

Bet grinned. "You've changed, Lou! I heard you, asking if I could come with you to Claremont. Thank you for facing Pa like that but I don't think he'll let me come with you. I'd love to go there – Dick says there's a great library where I could read and read. I don't know enough yet to be a teacher. One day, I shall have my own school." She took a small jar from her pocket. "Lou – I bought this from the pedlar."

This was just like Bet, see-sawing between jealousy and affection and I felt a pang of fondness for her as I looked at the jar. "What is it?"

Bet grinned. "It's a love potion. You smear it on your face, then go to the Holy Well at sunset and you'll see your future husband's reflection." She giggled "We'll creep out together and try it, just for fun." She hung her head in mock apology. "I'm sorry I sneaked on you but I did so want to go to the Fair."

She was jumping up and down with enthusiasm, her eyes gleaming with excitement instead of tears.

I couldn't disappoint her. "All right," I said. "But it's all nonsense, you know, like the fortune-teller." I slid the miniature into the pocket swinging from my belt and drew out the ribbon I'd bought for Bet. "Here you are – It'll go with your dark hair."

Bet hugged me. "Red's my favourite colour. And you'll ask again about my going with you to Claremont? After all, Dick's there, in the stables."

"I shan't go without you," I promised.

"And I won't tell about the miniature, our Lou-Lou."

I felt a nudging of guilt but I was resolved to keep the

painting.

It was one step further to finding out who I was.

CHAPTER 3

Bet waved her arms in the air dramatically and Tobias looked up, hoping she might throw him a tit-bit. "The main problem is, Lou, you're in the dog-house," she said. "No, not you, Toby-dog." She laughed at his anxious face.

We were back in my bedroom, where we could look out for Pa Edsir's return. I felt for the miniature in my pocket and the knowledge that I knew what my mother looked like, gave me new strength. I plaited the new red ribbon into Bet's curly dark hair and she preened herself at the looking-glass, wrapping her shoulders in my embroidered shawl – another present from the Tyrconnells. "I look at least sixteen," she said, arching her eyebrows and pursing her red lips. "Everyone thought I was the prettiest Queen of the May ever."

"You'll need a bigger bonnet for that swollen head," I teased and she threw a pillow at me.

Pictures of that happy day floated into my mind. It had been sunny and warm and I'd helped prepare a special meal before hurrying out with Mama Edsir and watching Bet garlanded with flowers on the farm cart – the church choir singing and the bells ringing to welcome in the spring. Two years before, I'd been Queen of the May and I'd never forgotten the excitement.

Tobias barked and we heard Billy's hooves in the yard. "Mama's back," I said. "I'll go downstairs and tell her I'm sorry if I upset her. I don't care about Pa, though but I'll stand up to him about us both going to Claremont."

Bet bounced on the bed, her skirt and shift riding up to show

25

her skinny legs.

"He'll be sending you back to your room, mind," she said. Then she jumped off the bed so suddenly that Tobias tore round the room with excitement, ears flapping and paws sliding on the floor. "Better go and help Ma," she said. "Maybe we can get her on our side."

Mrs. Edsir looked at me reproachfully as we crept into the kitchen. "You were supposed to stay in your room, dear."

"Lou's going to help me feed the hens," Bet said.

"Then I want to talk to Papa when he comes back," I said firmly. "I've not changed my mind. I am not going to Claremont without Bet."

I must have raised my voice because Annie woke up and creaked out of the old chair. Mama Edsir leaned on the kitchen table, as if she felt faint – as well she might because of the heat of the fire on a warm day. "You will have to ask Mr. Edsir again," she said. "I shall put in a good word for you, Lou, because it's kind of you to think of our Bet. I will certainly try to persuade him because Bet has the makings of a school-teacher, like me. I've taught you both all I know but I cannot make Young Ladies of you myself."

I hugged her impulsively. Mama Edsir had never made me feel different – she had treated me as fairly as all her other children.

She looked flushed but pleased. "I called on our Martha in the village. She's near her time and asked if you, Lou, could help with the little ones when she has the baby as she knows you love them."

"Certainly I will."

Our elder sister, Martha, as a teenager, was a second mother to Bet and myself and we missed her when she left to get married, even if it was only to live at the village forge. Bet and I often went over to help with the children.

Mrs Edsir remembered I had missed her mid-day dinner and insisted on giving me a slice of the newly baked bread,

26

smothered with our own butter. "I don't know what Mr. Edsir will say when he hears you disobeyed him," she said nervously. "I don't know what's got into you lately, Lou. You used to be such a quiet, obedient little girl."

I smiled at her. "I'm almost a woman now, you know."

"Pa won't be so cross if we help Daisy with the milking," Bet said. "Her sister's still away with a fever."

Mama agreed but still looked nervous.

When we got outside, I remembered the piglet. "Let's feed Bertha first, before he comes back." We put on our aprons and wooden patterns over our shoes – the farmyard was mucky at the best of times.

"Don't get too fond of her," Bet warned as we came to the old stable.

The piglet looked small and sad, curled in a corner, but as soon as we rattled the bucket, she came running and slurped at the milk and slops, grunting and twirling her tiny tail. Tobias stood on his hind legs, peering over the half-door.

"Pig-watching, girls?" Tom came into the stall, reeking of horses.

"Don't you think she'll be lonely here?" I asked him.

"She be only a pig!" He giggled. "She's eating well – in a couple of months she'll make good ham." He smacked his lips.

Bet gave him a push so he landed in the straw. "Tom – don't tease Lou. Can't you see she's gone all soft and motherly, like she does with anything baby? Remember she's not born of farming stock like us – as far as we know. Let's put her precious piglet in with Jess and her pups."

"I don't know what Pa will say to that," Tom said but I caught Bertha and we took her across the yard to the other stable where Jess, the sheepdog, lived with her pups. As soon as the half-door opened they rushed for Bertha. She squealed but stood her ground, ears flapping and tail up.

Jess sniffed at the piglet's nose, then spread herself on the

27

straw and the pups came running to feed. Bertha crept forward and pushed herself in, finding an empty teat. Jess grunted but didn't snap at her.

Tom laughed. "She's a real pig, wanting more after her feed."

We left them to it and went to the big barn next to the dairy where my eldest foster-brother William, was bringing in the cows to be milked. In the summer, the cows were milked in the field but it was easier in the barn next to the dairy.

William waved a greeting but he was a quiet man, only stopping to ask the milkmaid, Daisy, how her sister Marigold fared.

I found bucket and stool and sat down with my head against Ruby's warm flank. She was my favourite cow – not one for a sly inward kick which knocked the bucket over - and soon milk was gushing out of the her teats. The rhythmic action of my hands and the rich curdled scent of the cows and their milk were usually soothing, but I couldn't relax, thinking of Papa Edsir's return and the miniature I had virtually stolen.

Bet, on the next stool, leaned over and whispered, "I've an idea about tonight and how to get away to the Well."

I'd hoped she had forgotten. I didn't want to be in any more trouble.

The church clock was striking six by the time Papa Edsir clattered into the yard, throwing the reins to Tom and hurrying into the house, bellowing for his wife.

I'd been helping Bet and Annie prepare the usual light supper of bread, cheese and salads but as soon as Bet heard her father's voice, she took me by surprise, pulling me into the big larder by the kitchen door, Annie gawping as we went.

"We'll hear if he's in a good mood," she whispered.

We looked through a crack in the door as Mrs. Edsir peeked into the kitchen. "The Master's back, Annie," she called.

"We'll be eating when he's had his refreshment. I suppose the girls are upstairs?"

"She'll give us away," I whispered but Annie had one of her deaf fits on and just muttered something and I saw Mrs Edsir going out, leaving the door to the hall open.

I heard her saying, "Let me help take your boots off, my love. How fares the Duke?" She panted as she tugged at the boots – I supposed Farley Edsir must be sitting on the hall settle.

"Ah, that's better," he grunted. "My feet do swell these days. The Duke seems well, perhaps because he has his mistress with him at the moment as well as his wife."

"He's the King's brother, so I suppose he feels he can do what he wants. Now, dearest husband…" I imagined Mama carefully putting her hand on his arm, as if he were a dog that might bite.

"I do not wish to rile you, husband," she went on. "But Louisa still wants Bet to go with her to Claremont and I feel our Bet would benefit, if the Tyrconnells agree."

Mr. Edsir grunted. "So Louisa is still obstinate? The Tyrconnells want her to be educated because – well, you know why – they hope she will marry well, although that seems unlikely, with her lack of a dowry. We can't expect the money we receive to go on when she comes of age. I reckon even rich folk like them feel guilty because they know who abandoned her."

"Quiet, dear. Your voice is so loud." Mrs. Edsir now spoke with more force than she had ever done before. "I have talked to Louisa. She's quite determined Bet shall go with her. If the Countess agrees, Bet would have the chance to learn more. I don't think you realise, my love, that she is clever and might make a schoolteacher like me."

There was a silence then Mr. Edsir's voice rumbled on: "I can't understand it. Louisa has been so obedient up to now, never defying me."

"She's almost a woman, you know." Mama Edsir's voice was quiet but firm. "Although she's gentle and loving she also has a mind of her own and surely, that's for the good as she's on her own in the world."

"A strong-willed woman will never attract a good husband. And she will need a rich and well-connected man to satisfy them." He lowered his voice. "And You Know Who as well." He cleared his throat loudly. "If there's an opportunity, I might ask her Ladyship at church tomorrow if Bet can come with Louisa but I think she may refuse."

Bet clutched my arm in excitement.

"Thank you, husband." Mama was almost cooing now. There was a rustle and I wondered if she had kissed him.

"I need to talk to William tomorrow," Mr. Edsir said. "He says one of the cows has milk sickness and another is just about to calve. If only he still lived at home instead of walking here each day from Stoke, it would be easier."

"There's no room in this house now he has a wife and five children. Our Will works very hard for you, husband, far harder than the other men you employ."

I began to realise that Mama didn't always agree with her husband, even when he shouted at her. Up to now, I'd accepted that Mr. Edsir always got his way.

"Will is a good son, I agree. Now, wife, that ride's made me thirsty – I'll rest a while in my study and take refreshment before our meal." His voice faded as they both walked away.

"Ma's done it! She's brought him round," Bet said as we went back into the kitchen where Annie was already snoring in the old basket chair, an empty glass at her side.

The Edsirs' conversation had upset me but Bet was obviously thinking only of going to Claremont. "I shall wear my best muslin and bonnet for church and look as if butter won't melt in my mouth," she said.

I was feeling indignant. "Did you hear what Papa said? About needing a rich and well-connected husband for me, to satisfy them. I suppose he meant the Tyrconnells but also someone else."

"Oh, I heard that bit about 'you know who'. They must mean your father," Bet said.

"But they told me he'd been a soldier, who might have died, fighting those Americans."

As we walked out of the kitchen, Bet put her arm round me. "Best not to think about it. We're your family now. And wouldn't you like a rich husband? I would, to buy me a school to run. Not blooming well likely, though!"

"I'd like to ask him what he meant just now," I began.

"Let sleeping dogs lie," Bet whispered. "Let's make plans for tonight. You might very well see the face of your rich husband reflected in the Well."

CHAPTER 4

After supper, Dick came back from Claremont, looking hot and tired from the long walk. "Carter reminded me that I was lucky his Lordship let me home each night. The other stable-boys sleep in a stall, on straw."

"Like our little piggy," Bet giggled as we helped Annie clear the meal.

Dick turned round, looking at her. "I know you, young Bet. That look on your face. Are you planning something with Lou? Remember, she's a young lady now." There was a trace of bitterness in his voice.

"Why should we be planning anything?" Bet's face was blank and innocent. "And *I'll* be a young lady too soon – Pa is going to ask His Lordship if I can come to Claremont with Louisa and share the Governess with her and Lady Susan."

He laughed. "Then you'll be so high and mighty we won't be able to talk to you!" He laid his hand lightly on my shoulder. "I'm not too happy about my sisters going to the Big House. Carter let slip that he takes her Ladyship to Oatlands in the gig, quite often – to visit a very high-up personage. And as for her Ladyship's father, Lord Duval, he has a young lady-friend living nearby." He stopped.

"Oh, go on, Dick. Tell us some more!" Bet said but he strode out of the room.

We went to give Tobias a run in the field. House-martins swooped above us, getting ready to fly to warmer shores. I thought how brave they were – some said they flew as far as Africa. Did they pause, half way, and long to turn back?

Dick called us in. "You're to come to your beds, now, Ma says. Tom's fast asleep." He looked at the sky. "There'll be rain tonight – the birds are flying low."

"We won't see reflections in the well if it's raining," I whispered as we fetched candles and a jug of water for washing.

If I'd hoped to put Bet off, it had no effect.

"Oh, it won't rain. I know it in my bones." Bet said as she followed me into my bedroom. "Look, there's a grand sun-set."

We leaned out of the window and saw the great ball of the sun dip below the horizon, leaving streaks of orange, violet and blue. One of the Tyrconnells' presents had been a box of water-colour paints and I'd tried to capture a sunset without success – Bet said it my effort reminded her of eggs and bacon.

I wondered how I could put Bet off the visit to the Well. "You haven't said how we'll get out of the house. Papa bolts and locks the front and back door and takes the key to his room."

Bet gave me a push. "Are you getting too high and mighty to have fun? First I thought we'd climb down that thick old wisteria that grows below my bedroom window. Remember, we did it a year or so ago when we wanted to see the Guy Fawkes burned and Pa wouldn't let us?"

I looked at Tobias, lying half asleep on my bed. "If I shut him here on his own, he'll bark and he can't climb."

Bet grinned. "Then I thought of that, sis. Second idea – the larder window. I looked just now. It's big enough for us to get through."

The whole idea seemed daft to me but Bet's eyes were shining with excitement and it would be hard to disappoint her. Besides, I couldn't help remembering the gypsy's words and a tiny part of me longed to find out if I would ever marry even if the sensible part of me thought it was all superstitious rubbish. I didn't want to be the spinster daughter helping at the farm all my life. And I longed for a family of my own, babies that I would never desert.

"Why does time drag so slowly when you're waiting for something exciting, then rush along when you're enjoying yourself?" Bet complained. "I'd better go to my room in case Ma looks in to say goodnight."

I heard Annie thump up to her room, then I lay very still when Mama Edsir opened my door and peeped in before going to bed. Dick and Pa had a rumbling conversation in the corridor about the horses at Claremont and then all was quiet.

Bet slipped back to my room and we lay waiting for midnight, fully dressed, except for my tiresome stays. Tobias sleeping between us.

A barn-owl screeched outside and the Grandfather clock below struck eleven.

"Let's go early," Bet said. She took the precious candle in its jar and Tobias leaped down to follow us. It was impossible not to make a noise on the groaning ancient stair-treads and my heart thumped but Papa Edsir's loud snores still filled the silence.

It wasn't easy, getting out of the larder. First we had to move the big muslin-covered jugs of milk, standing in bowls of water against the heat. Tobias tried to jump up at the sight of the ham under its mesh but I held him tight.

Bet clambered up onto the marble shelf and slid quite easily through the narrow opening. She squealed as she landed. "Nettles" she gasped. "Come on."

I handed Bet the candle in its jar, then picked Tobias up and pushed him through the window into Bet's arms. I tried to follow but there was too much material in my thick skirt so I took it off, rolled it under my arm and climbed out wearing only my shift and my woollen stockings.

I tried not to scream as the nettles stung my arms.

The September night was cool but not cold and the full

moon had risen and silvered the garden so even the rows of cabbages gleamed. I thought how little we'd been allowed out at night, except for the Harvest Supper and Midnight service at Christmas and now I felt a strange magic in the air. We both looked in vain for dock leaves, then spat on our sore hands. Bats squeaked above our heads and big moths fluttered at the candle as Bet led the way out of the garden and down the lane, taking the turning that led to the river Mole.

I looked at the shining water. "It's like a silver ribbon."

"Doesn't the Mill look spooky?" Bet shivered, pointing. "Let's pretend there's a wicked magician living there, waiting to lure us in."

The tall mill building loomed over the river, its windows blind black eyes, and there was a creamy thread of water as the mill-wheel turned.

Tobias sniffed the air and pulled the rope out of my hands, leaping into the water after a sleeping duck. It rose in the air, leaving a circle of silver ripples. I called him back, and he came, shaking water all over me. I held tightly to his wet leash and scolded him so hard his long ears drooped sadly.

The moon darted in and out of dark clouds hiding the stars. The air was heavy and still, smelling of the river. Tobias stood still and looked back. Was that moving darkness someone following us?

"He's seen someone. Let's run," Bet said.

The Holy Well was away from the river, down a track between tall hedges, then through a kissing gate into a neighbouring farmer's field, where the sleeping cattle made dark smudges on the silvered grass. The bullocks got up when they saw Tobias and came after us, even though we shouted at them. They were were young and frisky, ready to chase a dog, so we fled down the hill, diving into the thicket surrounding the Holy Well.

Round the rough old wall surrounding the Well were hung crutches, mildewed bandages, tiny shoes, green with age and rough crosses made of twigs. I had heard of the Well but only Bet had been there before.

"Ma told me that long ago, the Priest made money out of sick people coming here to pray for healing," she said. "Now folk sometimes throw pennies down and pray for their crops or good husbands. The plague pit's nearby and they say the ghosts of the dead walk at midnight." Her voice was dramatic, echoing into the dark hole of the well.

I shivered and then was annoyed with myself. I was too old to believe all these stories – but all the same…

Bet asked me to hold the candle while she spread evil-smelling ointment on our faces. Then she told me to look down.

Tobias whined and pulled at the lead. I let him go and told him to wait. To please my young sister, I looked into the well. The water-level was only a few feet from the top and we could see our pale faces reflected in the candlelight.

Then Bet shrieked. A white face lit by an uncanny light hovered over us, a face whose eyes were dark caverns.

CHAPTER 5

I couldn't move.

Strong hands gripped my shoulders. "Don't be daft. It's me," said Dick. "What are you two doing here at night? You could be attacked by beggars or worse. Come home at once." I wanted to giggle hysterically when I saw he was wearing an old coat over his nightshirt.

He marched us back through the fields and along the path to the river. "I heard you scuffling downstairs and thought you were robbers. I was just in time to see you go to the river and into the field, then Tobias came running and led me to the Well."

Bet's voice was soft, pleading. "Please don't tell."

"I'll think about it." The moon had disappeared behind clouds so he swung the oil-lamp towards us. "What's that white stuff on your faces?"

Bet said something but her voice was drowned by a crash of thunder followed by lightning, then the rain fell, hitting us hard as rods. Dick hurried us along but we were all soaked by the time we reached the farm.

He had a key to the back door and said it was a spare, so he could come and go as he wished.

As we dripped our way in and tried to creep upstairs, a voice bellowed: "Who's there? I'm armed!"

Dick pushed us flat in the shadow of the stair wall and leaped ahead, two steps at a time.

Papa Edsir was on the landing, wearing his striped nightshirt and a nightcap and holding an ancient pistol.

When he saw Dick he lowered it. "What are you doing? It's nearly midnight and you're soaking wet."

What would Dick say? I hardly dared breathe. I put my hand over Tobias' muzzle to keep him from whining.

"Sorry to wake you, Pa," Dick said. "But I thought I heard a noise outside and I went to see – got wet too, running outside, but there wasn't anyone there. You go back to bed or we'll wake Ma and Tom."

I heard Papa Edsir muttering something about the dogs not barking and then a door shutting.

"Hurry." Dick whispered, almost dragging us up the stairs. "And don't do it again," he said sternly as we went to our rooms.

I took off my wet shift and did my best to dry myself and Tobias with the rough towel from the wash-stand. Then, shivering, I covered the dog and myself with the quilt.

So, it was Dick's face I had seen in the reflection. But of course it was just a silly superstition. As I drifted into sleep, I thought how kind Dick was and how safe I'd felt when he had his hands on my shoulders. Perhaps...

I was woken by Mama Edsir gently shaking my shoulder. "You have over-slept, Lou dear." Tobias poked his head out of the bedclothes. "And don't let Mr. Edsir see the dog on your bed. I've run the flat-iron over your best dress. Hurry up, or you'll be late for church."

She went out before she could see the wet shift hanging on the chair.

It was all hustle and bustle downstairs and I was thankful I had a clean shift to put on under my best muslin dress and bonnet.

The dog-cart being too small for all of us, Dick hitched Billy to the farm wagon with its hard wooden seats. The Tyrconnells would arrive in a coach and sit on soft cushioned seats, and I couldn't help envying them.

The sun was a pale disc gleaming through thick mist but at

least it wasn't raining. Last night's silly adventure almost forgotten, I wondered if I ought to go to church without confessing to Mama Edsir I'd taken the miniature?

When we got to our usual pew, I saw that most of the Edsir family were at the church – Martha, big with child, and her husband Jed, sister Mary and brother James with his wife and family. They'd all been kind and loving towards me most of my life – they *were* my life – so why did I feel so restless and incomplete?

"Lucky Will – having to stay behind and tend that sick cow," Bet whispered. She grew easily bored with the long prayers and sermon.

The Tyrconnells came in late, coming through the side door into their special pew but of course the Rector had waited the service for them. The Countess, pretty Lady Sarah, was dressed in the finest white muslin and wore her fair hair piled up under her enormous feathered hat. She was very thin and coughed as she took her seat. Dick said she had an affliction of the lungs that no doctor could cure.

"She's wearing rouge and lip-salve," Bet whispered. Beside her, Lord Tyrconnell looked almost as old as the grandfather, Lord Delaval, who sat with a slim, delicate-looking girl I'd heard was hoping to be the third Lady Delaval.

The governess was there, a tall, thin woman dressed in mourning black with the Tyrconnells' teenage daughter, Lady Susan, who smiled when she saw us. She was always friendly when they visited the farm but her mother looked at me strangely and made me feel uncomfortable.

I'd seen the governess before and thought she looked sad but not fierce, like the village schoolmistress who rapped our hands with her cane. I told myself it was no use thinking of lessons with her unless Bet could come too.

The sun shone through the church's one stained glass window, making patterns on the aisle floor. I dreamed my way through the service, imagining my mother coming to this church, expecting the baby she couldn't keep. I had the paper folded round the miniature in my pocket. "Look after Louisa Maria." She must have hated to part with her baby.

"So boring," Bet whispered as the Rector again thundered out an old sermon..

Several of the congregation had fallen asleep after an hour but they woke up when Tom, caught yet again playing with his pet mouse, had been taken out of the church in disgrace.

When we came out at the end of the service, the Tyrconnells and Lord Duval were already there, nodding graciously when the villagers filed past, bobbing a curtsy and doffing caps.

"As if they're Royalty," Bet whispered.

I suddenly felt a sympathy for those poor French peasants, rebelling against the very rich. Then I remembered the execution of the King and Queen of France and so many others and shuddered.

Lady Tyrconnell put out a small gloved hand. "Louisa – I hope you are coming to Claremont to study with Miss Wildbore?"

I curtsied. "I thank your Ladyship. I wonder if I might bring my sister, Elizabeth? She's eager to learn and wants to become a school-teacher."

Bet curtsied and put on her best and dimpled smile.

"Why not, Mama?" Susan said. "The more the merrier."

I thought I saw her wink at Bet – a very unladylike thing to do.

Lady Tyrconnell looked doubtful as she turned to the governess. "Miss Wildbore – what do you think? It will only be until October when we go to our London house."

"If your Ladyship wishes, I would agree." Miss Wildbore's voice was soft and meek.

Lady Tyrconnell nodded vaguely, as if she had lost interest. "Tomorrow, then. Dick will bring you both." Then she began to cough again and left, with an elegant wave of her small gloved hand.

Mr. Edsir was bowing and smiling but as soon as the Tyr-connells had gone, he turned on me. "You were very forward, Miss, instead of waiting for me, Bet's father, to speak for her."

I tried to look sorry but it was yet another time when I felt Mr. Edsir did not really care for me.

As soon as we were home we ran upstairs to take off our gloves and bonnets. Bet hugged me and whirled me around until I was dizzy. "Lou – you're the best sister I have. And just think, we'll be taught by a Wild Boar!" She fell on the bed, giggling. "What a name to have!"

"I thought a governess would be stiff and strict," I said. "She looks…" I was going to say, "sad" but Bet interrupted me.

"Like a dog that's been whipped too often!"

Now my sister was coming with me, I forgot my fears and longed to see the great house and the beautiful grounds Dick had described.

Perhaps there might be a clue there to the secret of my birth.

CHAPTER 6

"Oh, it's so grand!" Bet exclaimed as we drove to the imposing building. Ornate iron railings led up to a big door but Dick said that was the back of the house. "Since you're preparing to be young ladies, I'll take you to the front," he said urging Billy round the building to where a grand sweep of driveway led up to the stone columns on either side of the huge front door.

Dick had described the house simply as "big", being more interested in the stables and the number of loose-boxes. I felt a little nervous, staring up at the glittering glass in the many windows. I wondered who might be looking out at our old horse and battered cart and for a disloyal moment I wished we'd come in a brand new trap, drawn by a high-stepping horse.

Lady Susan must have seen us coming because she ran down the steps.

"Welcome!" She was smiling at us. "Don't worry about our Butler, Sampson," She waved her hand at the glum-faced man, grandly dressed, who stood by the open front door. "He prefers to announce visitors and thinks I'm quite mad, dashing out like this!"

She smiled at Dick, who raised his cap and drove round to the stables.

I was glad I had left Tobias behind for once when two large grey dogs rose to meet us. Growling softly, they sniffed at me and then wagged their tails.

"Wolfhounds," Lady Susan said. "They look fierce but

they're really friendly."

Miss Wildbore, still wearing black, joined us in the vast hall. We both bobbed a curtsey, not being sure of the right way to greet a governess.

She smiled nervously, saying, "Welcome, girls," in a whispery voice.

I was staring round the hall with its beautiful staircase and big chandeliers, dripping glittering glass diamonds.

"Should we go to the schoolroom, Lady Susan?" Miss Wildbore asked.

"I just want to show them the dining hall first." Susan led us to a great room with richly patterned carpet, a myriad family portraits hanging on the walls and huge dining-table. "It's my favourite room after my bedchamber," she said.

"You could get the whole village into here!" Bet said.

"You should see Seaton Delaval – my grandfather's house in Northumberland," Lady Susan boasted. "It's bigger and better. Then of course we have two houses in London, although we may have to shut them up after all this trouble with the Bank of England. Boring economies. I have no new dress for the summer, for instance and my grandfather's lady-friend, Miss Knight, says she has been instructed not to buy any more kid gloves. Mind, she already has ten pairs." She laughed.

"Susan – I don't think your parents would want you to discuss money in this vulgar way," Miss Wildbore said.

"Lady Susan's a show-off," Bet whispered to me but I was looking at the portraits, just wondering if the face on the miniature might be one of them but I didn't recognise any of them.

Miss Wildbore was hurrying after Bet, who had gone to examine the carvings on the dining-chairs. "Don't touch, dear. We don't want finger-marks on the polish," she said. I thought a little indignantly that she imagined Bet would have dirty hands, just because she came from a farm.

43

Susan was close by. I found I was breathing fast but I had to ask. "Could I show you something, Lady Susan?" I took the miniature from my pocket. "Have you ever seen a portrait of this lady?"

She looked surprised but examined the small painting. "She's beautiful. I think I saw her once – when I was younger. I had been sent to bed for misbehaviour – as I often am!" She laughed. "But I heard the dogs bark and this lady was in the hall. Then Sampson took her into my father's study. Our old nursemaid chased me to bed so I didn't see her again. Nobody mentioned her in the morning and I forgot about her until now."

I saw Bet turning to stare at me as I summoned up my courage. "As you know, your family has always brought me gifts so I wondered if they knew my mother. Perhaps she might have been a distant relation? I was told she died when I was a baby."

Susan looked at me and frowned. "I'm so sorry, Louisa. I've asked my parents before why we give presents to you, and I was told it was a family secret and an obligation from the past."

I hated the thought of being 'an obligation' but I didn't reply as Miss Wildbore led us to a back staircase to the top floor. "This is the schoolroom," she announced.

It was an oak-panelled room with three desks, quills, paper and ink and a big globe of the world.

"Books!" Bet whispered, pointing to the crowded shelves.

Miss Wildbore adjusted her frilly cap with a darting, nervous gesture and asked us to sit down. She stood, smiling uneasily. "Now, I would like to know what you, Miss La Coast, and Miss Edsir have learned already. I have been instructed to give you both elocution and deportment lessons but Lady Susan is enjoying acting parts of William Shakespeare's plays…"

Susan interrupted, I thought rudely. "I want to be an actress.

My mama has acted in plays at our other house – she was a wonderful Desdemona and I take after her. Of course, my parents disapprove – they want me to be quiet and ladylike and marry some boring Earl or Duke."

Miss Wildbore looked at her reproachfully. "Now, we've discussed this before, Lady Susan. As you say, your parents..." she hesitated.

"They wouldn't mind if I was like the famous actress Mrs. Jordan, the Duke of York's other lady-love." Lady Susan gave a sly smile. "No wonder our poor King goes mad – worrying about both his brothers' affairs."

I was amazed that she could interrupt a teacher and talk so wildly.

Miss Wildbore thumped so hard on Lady Susan's desk that I jumped but Susan just giggled.

"No more talk like this, Lady Susan. The girls have come here to learn."

Susan gave a huge sigh, giving us a sideways look. I'd always envied her looks and clothes. She had unusually large green eyes and a mass of ringlets, the colour of ripe chestnuts, artfully framing her face, so unlike my unruly red curls. "You'll want to see me acting Shakespeare, won't you, girls?" she asked. "You can read a part, if you wish."

Bet's rosy face glowed. "Yes, please, my Lady," she said eagerly. "Lou and me often used to make up little plays."

It sounded so childish. "When we were younger," I said quickly.

Susan recited passionately from Romeo & Juliet, taking the part of Romeo and Bet acted Juliet, standing on a chair. "Just pretend it's a balcony," she ordered. "All you say is "Wherefore art thou, Romeo?"

Bet did her best, trying to look love-lorn and not to giggle as Susan knelt on the floor, declaiming her love.

"Again, with more feeling!" Susan ordered Bet, who almost shouted the lines. The chair wobbled and she fell off. Susan

45

laughed. "Plenty of feeling there but you sound as if you're calling in the cows."

I knew Bet would be hurt so I frowned at Susan but she was giggling as she tried to help Bet up but my sister pushed her away angrily.

"Lady Susan, please remember your manners." Miss Wildbore's voice was tired. I guessed she had given up trying to curb Susan's high spirits and forthright way of speaking.

Bet snapped back, "I beg pardon, Lady Susan, if my country voice offends. But I don't mind what you think – I am going to be a head-mistress of a girls' school and they'll learn more than acting, deportment and water-colour painting. Interesting things." She looked at the globe of the world. "About far-away places, history, new inventions, science…"

"Bet!" I whispered, beckoning her to sit down. If she went on like this Miss Wildbore might refuse to teach her.

Lady Susan clapped her hands. "Bravo! I like a girl with spirit. We women have to show what we can do."

Those fleeting visits of the Tyrconnells to the farm hadn't shown me what Susan was really like.

Miss Wildbore sighed. "I once had ambition." Her voice was so low I barely heard it. "But we have to remember our place in life. I shall be teaching you botany as well as embroidery, painting and music."

Bet slumped down in her seat beside me, red-faced, embarrassed. I was amazed – my younger sister had never told me her ambitions before. I nudged her. "Say you are sorry," I muttered.

"Sorry to offend, Miss Wildbore and My Lady," Bet whispered. "But I was speaking from my heart."

Miss Wildbore smiled. "Remember, I am supposed to teach you two girls how to become young ladies, Elizabeth. I myself taught in a small Dame school until my Mother died and her cottage had to be sold. Then…" She cleared her throat.

46

"Now, girls, a lesson on deportment." She made us put books on our heads and walk up and down the room. Bet kept giggling and her book slid off.

"Watch me!" Susan said, twirling round so fast that her book shot off and swept the ink and quills off a desk. She laughed and didn't offer to clear it up, instead ringing a bell and a thin little servant-girl came with a bucket and cloth.

After this, Miss Wildbore hesitantly suggested sketching in the gardens but Susan said it was time to exercise her mare and the governess meekly agreed.

"I don't suppose you two can ride?" Susan said in a patronizing voice.

"Yes," I said quickly.

"Lou rides on our Billy but I don't care for it," Bet said. "I'll go sketching, Miss. I want to see them beautiful gardens."

"Those," Miss Wildbore corrected but she looked pleased.

They went off to the gardens followed by a very young black boy weighed down by a stool and easel.

Susan looked at me doubtfully. "I would lend you one of my riding habits but I think I'm taller and more mature in figure than you." She preened herself, thrusting out her curves, showing off as usual.

I thought of the times I had sneaked a bareback ride on Billy. "I'm certainly slimmer than you, your Ladyship." I knew I sounded rude but I didn't care. Susan might be titled but she needed taking down a peg or two.

She changed into a smart black riding habit, edged with a thin line of red satin. I felt a pang of jealousy, clumbered as I was with my best wool skirt.

Dick was called from cleaning the brass on the coach and asked to saddle up Susan's mare, Juno, and a mare called Folly for me.

I smiled at Dick and hoped he wouldn't tell Susan that I'd never ridden side-saddle before.

He looked concerned. "Your Ladyship – Folly might

become a little frisky because she's not been ridden lately."

Susan smiled at him, showing her dimples and small white teeth. She took no notice of his words. "Saddle Folly, at once, Dick," she repeated, this time with a flirtatious look which I disliked.

"Carter's asked me to exercise his Lordship's horse," he said. "I can follow, to see if Lou – I mean Miss La Coast – is happy with Folly. She's never ridden a big horse before." He gave me a warning look and I knew he'd lecture me when we got home.

Susan waved her arm dismissively. "Oh, if you like. Brothers can be protective, can't they, Miss La Coast?"

I thought Dick leaned too close to Susan as he helped her mount her bay mare. I watched carefully as she curved one knee gracefully round the pommel of the saddle, and carefully arranged her smart riding-habit.

There was a mounting-block but Dick muttered, "I'll help you up, Lou," and before I could protest he had grasped me under the arms and plonked me firmly in the saddle, giving me whispered instructions on how to hold the double reins and hook my right leg over the pummel of the side-saddle.

"Sit up straight," he hissed. I was mortified to see my skirt was bunched up, showing a length of ugly worsted stocking.

Folly stood quietly but she was more than a hand taller than old Billy, and I felt insecure, missing the contact of the horse's sides between my knees.

Dick went to saddle another horse for himself.

Lady Susan and her mare were impatient to leave. "Come on. We don't need to wait for your brother, do we, Louisa?" she called as she clattered out of the stable-yard.

Folly immediately trotted after Juno. I thought the saddle felt very hard after riding bareback and it was so strange, sitting with my legs on the same side of the mare.

"I'm so tired of riding in the park – let's go to the Heath," Susan said.

We trotted at speed down the driveway, scattering a herd of deer. I saw the gleam of a lake but I was too busy coping with the unfamiliar horse to look round any further.

We were out on the dusty road now and the horses laid back their ears and shied sideways as a mail coach thundered past from Portsmouth.

Juno was ahead, just turning off into a muddy lane when Folly suddenly stretched her neck out, almost pulling the reins from my hands, cantering past Juno and then galloping down a sandy track winding through silver birch trees and purple heather.

The sun was shining, and it was wonderful to be riding down an unknown lane at such a speed but I realised too late that the mare had a hard mouth and could hardly feel me pulling the reins.

When I realised Susan and Juno were far behind, I began to feel scared. I clutched at Folly's mane and the pommel for dear life, then tried leaning right back and pulling on the reins as hard as I could but the mare took no notice.

Suddenly I saw a horseman cantering across the ride in front of me.

"Help me, Sir," I called. "I can't stop!"

I saw a quick flash of bright uniform as he rode up to Folly, reaching for the reins.

The stop was too abrupt and I shot off, landing with a painful thud on my shoulder, my skirts flying over my head, so for a moment I was fighting the folds of material. I heard flying hooves as Folly pulled away and galloped for home.

CHAPTER 7

"Are you hurt?" He had dismounted and was bending over me.

"No." My voice was muffled by my skirts. Worse than my bruised shoulder, was the knowledge that he could see my shift and even my stockings and garters. I managed to pull down my skirt, hot with embarrassment. Then I saw he had turned politely away.

I was struggling up but before I could protest, strong hands were pulling me up and for a moment, we stood close. Looking up at this handsome giant – for he must be well over six feet tall, I wondered where I had seen him before. And why was my body tingling so strangely at his touch?

"You have part of the woods in your beautiful hair – may I?"

Before I could protest he was carefully removing twigs and leaves. Nobody had ever before complimented me on my hair and I knew I was as scarlet as his coat.

He released his hold and I stepped back. "You know, I've seen you before." He smiled. "I caught your shuttlecock when it flew over the wall as I rode past. To be truthful, I was hoping I might see you again. I kept remembering your lovely face."

Had he been following me or was it just a coincidence? I tried not to smile back but his deep voice was warm and almost seductive and I had to admit, I enjoyed his compliment.

"I thank you, Sir, for helping on both occasions." I hoped my formal manner would show I was no empty-headed flirt.

Then I looked down the track, dismayed. "My mare, Folly, has gone! And she's only loaned to me."

He frowned. "Folly is aptly named! I'm so sorry – she pulled the reins out of my hands as I dismounted and I was too concerned for you to go after her."

Surely Lady Susan and Dick would catch up with me very soon? I realised Folly had bolted with me quite a long way.

There we were, in this secluded glade of silver-birch trees. This man was a stranger. Anything could happen – and my reputation might be ruined.

He smiled at me. "Please don't look so afraid." He took my hand again, gently. "I'm Captain Godfrey Macdonald, back from fighting in the Low Countries and going to Bagshot Heath for the Army manoeuvres. Might I ask your name?"

"Louisa Edsir, Sir." I refused to give the other stupid name. "I'm with Lady Susan Carpenter from the Tyrconnells' house, Claremont. The groom, my brother Dick, is with her. I shall just walk back to meet them."

I began to walk away but my hip was painfully bruised as well as my shoulder and I was mortified to find I was limping.

He caught up with me easily. "You're shaken and bruised. Let me take you back on my horse, Miss Edsir." He must have seen my expression for he added, "I'll lead him, of course."

For a wild moment, I thought how I'd like to sit in front of him but I told myself not to be silly. "It's good of you, Sir…" Why was I stammering?

"You are quite safe with me, I promise," he said. "Let me help you mount. Brutus is well trained, unlike your mare, but I am afraid you'll have to sit astride."

I had to accept – I just couldn't walk very far at the moment. "Thank you, Sir. I'm used to sitting astride. That side-saddle made me feel unsafe."

Near me again, he smelled of the open air, clean linen and faintly, but not unpleasantly, of his own musky scent. He was so tall – he made me feel small and fragile. My heart beat

51

faster as he lifted me into the saddle and I smoothed down my skirts. I felt a long way from the ground.

"Do you live with these Tyrconnells, Miss Edsir?" he asked, looking up at me as he led the horse slowly along.

He probably thought I was some kind of companion or servant. "No – my sister and I have lessons with their governess. I live on a farm a few miles away."

"A farmer's daughter?"

I supposed he would think less of me but I went on, "The Edsirs are my foster-parents." I thought I would change the conversation. "So you've been away, fighting, Captain Macdonald?"

"It was perhaps an ill-considered invasion of the Low Countries and we were defeated." He sighed.

"I shouldn't like to fight – to kill someone." I always hated to hear of wars and bloody revolutions.

"Soldiers have to kill – or be killed." His voice was thoughtful. "I have had my own doubts, sometimes, but at the moment, it's my career."

He had taken off his hat and as he looked up at me, I couldn't help noticing his thick fair hair, neatly plaited back and his big blue eyes.

"So what of your life, Miss Edsir?" he asked. "Do you have a secret longing?"

He was a stranger and yet he'd asked me a very intimate question. "I've never been away from Surrey," I said slowly. "I'd like to travel, to see London, or go north as far as Scotland. Perhaps even to go abroad… I like being on the farm but…"

"You feel restricted."

"Yes."

He patted my horse's neck and I saw he wore a gold signet ring.

"As you are such a beautiful girl, I'm afraid you will be engaged to marry before you have time to travel." He smiled

52

up at me.

My face was hot again, partly with pleasure but doubt crept in – was it right that a stranger should flatter me like this? I decided to be blunt and tell him the truth. "I have no dowry and in any case, I don't want to marry until I am older."

He laughed. "I don't think lack of a dowry would put off any determined suitor. Unless, of course, you approve of all these arranged marriages, for money and titles?"

"I certainly don't believe in arranged marriages. I would only ever marry for love."

Had I really said that and to a stranger?

"That's exactly how I feel," he said. "Love is all-important."

He laughed. "I have to confess I have met many pretty girls but I've never been in love."

I tried to change the subject. "I expect you have been very occupied with military matters."

"True. After our training at Bagshot Heath I'm to be sent to Ireland in the New Year, with a different regiment."

Why did I feel just a pang of regret? We were poles apart, socially.

I gabbled on, nervously. "That will be a new century – 1800. It sounds so strange. My sister Bet says we shall be modern women and she hopes to be a teacher. My foster-parents and the Tyrconnells want me to become a Young Lady, which is silly if I am to stay at the farm."

"Are your parents dead, then?" he began but he was interrupted by the thud of hooves on the soft turf. As they came round the bend, Dick, riding a grey mare and leading Folly on a rein, was cantering towards them followed by Lady Susan on Juno.

"Lou!" Dick shouted, pulling the horses up abruptly. "What happened? And who is this gentleman?" His voice was cold and almost rude.

"Dick, this is Captain Macdonald who rescued me – he stopped Folly from bolting but then I fell off..." My voice tailed off at their looks of disapproval.

Lady Susan was now beside Dick. "Perhaps you had better get off the Captain's horse now, Louisa." Her voice was cold. "Dick, please help her dismount."

Dick was off his horse and almost pushing the Captain away to help me down.

I knew why Susan and Dick were angry but all the same, the Captain had rescued me so there was no need to be rude. "Thank you, Sir," and I remembered my manners, and curtsied.

He smiled. "It was a pleasure, Miss Louisa." Then he raised his hat to Lady Susan, remounted and galloped away.

"How could you, Lou!" Dick said in a furious whisper.

Lady Susan was frowning. "He's certainly very handsome and so tall. But you shouldn't have allowed him…"

I interrupted, "I had no choice." I wanted to defend him. "If he hadn't been there, I don't know where Folly would have taken me. Does she often bolt like that?"

Susan didn't answer but Dick said, "Yes – if she senses an uncertain rider." He looked almost defiantly at Susan. "Your Ladyship, I did warn you. Folly was unsuitable for my sister."

I almost held my breath. I knew how much Dick's job at the stables meant to him. Servants were often dismissed for defiant or impudent behaviour.

Lady Susan looked startled, as if no servant had questioned her judgement before. Then she said, "I thought Miss La Coast had ridden often but obviously only on a farm-horse and without a side-saddle." Again she was patronising but she added, "I'm sorry, Louisa. You will have to practise on my old pony – if you aren't too badly shaken."

I hated to be thought a coward and I spoke firmly. "A fall won't frighten me away from riding. Please help me mount Folly again, Dick."

He seemed rigid with angry disapproval and insisted on walking beside me, holding leading Folly and his own horse.

I was surprised to see the stable yard clock, showing it was half-past two. I was hungry, having missed the mid-day meal at the farm but Mr. Edsir had warned us both that the Tyrconnells dined at three and would not want company.

"You will need to rest at home, Louisa." Susan ordered Dick to harness Billy.

Bet was in raptures on the journey home. "Oh, Lou! I want to live there, at Claremont. It's so beautiful and do you know, when I asked for the privy I found they had more than one and indoors. They don't need a well and there's running water and a strange kind of marble bath place below stairs and we went to the lake where I drew a sketch. There's a little house on an island where they sometimes have parties and a Belvedere, that's a big tower. Miss W. said the gentlemen played cards there but I think there's probably a mad relation shut up there or ghosts. And we went down a grassy bowling alley. I can't wait to play ninepins. Miss W. and I found several unusual plants and flowers to press – she knows all the Latin names – she says she hopes we will return. I think she's lonely. And she's far too gentle for that show-off head-strong Lady Susan."

She stopped to take a breath. "Oh, and how did you enjoy your ride?"

"It was – exciting." I shifted my seat to relieve the bruises.

Dick sat in front of them, driving Billy, silent and disapproving.

I remembered the Captain's kindness and the warmth of his hands. But of course, he was an Army officer and I was only the adopted daughter of a farmer. Also, it was likely he would soon be rejoining his Regiment abroad so I was unlikely to see him again. I had to put him out of my mind.

"Actually, Bet, I must confess my mare bolted," I said. Then, because Dick was listening I added, "Fortunately, an officer rode across our path and stopped her but I fell off. We saw this soldier before – that time when he rode past and caught our shuttlecock."

Bet's mouth opened wide. "I can't believe it! He was so handsome."

I had to spare Dick's feelings. "Oh, I hardly noticed," I said quckly.

When we arrived home, Dick said he had to walk back the three miles to Claremont to tend the horses. He stalked off, without a smile.

We unharnessed Billy and set him loose in the field.

As soon as we came into the house, we heard a great wailing and weeping coming from the kitchen. Annie was sitting with her shawl over her face, rocking back and forth.

"Whatever is it?" Bet asked her.

It was hard to hear her but eventually her muffled voice said, "Missus has told me to go and no reference. Nobody will employ me as a servant because she says I am a thief and I never touched her box. She says I stole a valuable miniature when I was dusting the sewing room."

I felt sick and the room swirled round me.

I had to confess.

CHAPTER 8

"Could you please fetch Mama, Bet, while I comfort Annie," I said. "I'll tell her the truth."

"You'll be in real trouble this time," Bet said.

"Doesn't matter." I gently took the shawl off the old lady's head. "Annie – I'm so sorry you were blamed. I took the miniature because I think it belongs to me anyway. There was a note, too."

"You took it, Louisa!" Mama came into the kitchen with Bet. "You have been in my private box and now poor Annie has been blamed for thieving." Unusually, she sounded really angry. "Please give it to me before Mr. Edsir finds out."

I clutched the miniature in my pocket. I was glad I had put the treasured piece of paper in my prayer-book upstairs. "No! I'm sorry I didn't ask you if I could have it but I think the portrait is of my mother."

"Only because you saw the note with your name." Mama said, her face red, her words tumbling out, confused. "That's – just a miniature I was given."

Old Annie was staring, open-mouthed.

"Are you sure?" My voice rose. "Why don't you tell me the truth? Why can't I know my mother's name and my father's?"

"I can't believe this of you, Lou." Mrs. Edsir's kind face was pinched with worry as she came into the kitchen, hearing the loud talking. "I don't know what Mr. Edsir will say."

"Oh, don't tell Pa!" Bet said.

"Fancy you letting me be blamed like that so I'd lose my place." Annie muttered angrily.

"It's all a misunderstanding. You go to your room, Annie, and have a rest." Mrs. Edsir's voice was soothing and Annie tottered off, but still muttering.

When she had gone, Bet clutched at Mama's arm. "Ma – as she says, Lou thinks it might be her mother's face portrayed in that miniature. So it's rightly hers."

I stood quite still. After my confession, I didn't know what to say. Then I again felt a welling up of unusual anger. "It is a portrait of my mother, isn't it?" I was mortified to find my voice was trembling. "And she wrote a note when I was left with you?"

Mrs. Edsir sank back into the basket-chair as if her legs had given way. "Yes," she whispered.

"So it is mine, by rights?"

Mama didn't answer.

"So – what was her name?" I actually shouted out the words, exploding from the years of her refusing to answer my questions.

"Lou!" Bet hissed. "Don't yell at Ma."

Mrs. Edsir looked up, her lace cap slipping almost over one eye. Her voice was low and anguished. "I'm bound not to tell you. But I think of you as one of my own. And please give me back the miniature – I shall keep it safe. Mr. Edsir will be angry if he finds you have it." Tears trickled down her nose.

I felt some shame that I had hurt the only mother I knew. "Why should he be angry? I don't want to hurt you, Mama, but I shall keep the miniature."

"I made a promise." Mrs Edsir's voice was muffled by her tears.

I knelt by her and put my head into that ample lap. "You know I love you as a mother," I said. "And I'm happy here. But I'm almost a woman now and I need to find out the secret. Are my parents alive or dead? If they're alive, why haven't they come to see me?" Tears spilled down my cheeks.

Mrs. Edsir stroked my hair. "I'm so sorry, dear child. But we

58

long ago swore to keep the names secret."

The front door banged and Tobias was barking.

Mr. Edsir's loud voice boomed, "Wife! I am back! Where are you?"

"I have to go to him." Mrs. Edsir hurried out and I heard them talking in the hall and then footsteps, going upstairs.

"She'll be helping him take off his boots now he's so stout," Bet said. "Best hide that miniature. Though I doubt our mother would search your room." She put her arm round my waist. "Have you thought, Lou, that it might be better not to know about your parents? I mean, they've never bothered to see you. Our ma loves you like her own and I love you like a sister."

I couldn't explain my frustration, even to my much-loved foster-sister. Bet had proper parents and I didn't. Finding the miniature had stirred up questions and brought back that sense of not belonging anywhere.

Bet was sniffing. "That bucket of pig-swill smells something rotten. Think how hungry our Bertha must be. Let's feed her."

I knew Bet was trying to distract me so I followed her outside.

The sheep-dog was asleep but the piglet rushed up to the half-door with the pups behind her, so we had to push them back as we filled the pig's little trough, which she emptied in a quick guzzle. Then we sat in the straw, the piglet nuzzling us and the three pups trying to chew our skirts. Tobias stood on his hind legs, trying to look over the half door and whining that he was left out.

I tried to calm myself, looking at the animals, but I couldn't forget what had been said.

Tom found us there. "Rector's just called. You're both wanted in the parlour," he said.

"We smell of pig," Bet whispered as we washed our hands under the pump. I pinned up my hair and put on the frilly cap which always irritated me.

"The Rector will have to put up with the smell," I said. "Bertha's one of God's creatures, after all." He was the last person I wanted to see at the moment, my thoughts all tumbling about as they were.

Mama was sitting very upright and proper in the stuffy un-used parlour, facing our plump Rector, who heaved himself out of his chair when he saw us. "Ah, Louisa and Elizabeth, I have come to tell you that the Lord Bishop is now recovered, thank God, and will confirm you both in three week's time."

As I curtsied respectfully, I thought the Reverend Wadham Diggle, with his big mouth and protruding eyes, looked a little like an anxious frog as he added, "Do you feel you need more instruction?"

"No thank you, Sir!" We spoke together. The Reverend Diggle once a week was bad enough.

He paused. "I hear from your mother, Miss Louisa, that you and Elizabeth have been to Claremont House to study with the Lady Susan Carpenter, daughter of the Earl. You are most privileged and it must be of great benefit."

We looked at each other, trying not to laugh. It was well known. that the Rector loved anybody with a title.

"We've only just started there, Sir," I said.

The Rector gave us two prayer books. "My wife sends her regards and hopes Miss Louisa continues her music and also her painting and sketching, for which I gather she has some ability. I believe I fostered her interest in poetry and literature, to some extent." He began to smile at me but suddenly sniffed and blew his nose. I feared he had smelled the piglet on our clothes.

Bet was trying to hide her smiles as I thanked the Rector.

As soon as he had gone, Mrs. Edsir was all smiles, as if the scene earlier in the kitchen had never happened. "I shall have to make you both Confirmation dresses. Silk would be expensive but muslin will do nicely."

Bet smiled. "Oh, don't worry about our Lou, Ma. Tell the

Tyrconnells about the Confirmation and they'll send over a pure silk dress for her."

"There's no need to talk like that, Bet." Mrs. Edsir frowned. "The family have been very generous. And, Louisa, I have thought carefully – you may keep the miniature and I shall not tell Mr. Edsir about it."

I gave her a hug.

Mrs. Edsir sniffed loudly. "Child, you smell of the byre! Be off and wash."

At supper, Mr. Edsir looked tired. "There is much for me do at Hampton Court," he said, sighing. "His Majesty, King George, is to come on a visit and the Duke expects me to attend to many details in the household, from food to stabling."

"Your father has a very important position as Steward to the Duke." Mama reminded us, as she had many times before.

"We have never seen the Palace, Pa," Bet said. "Could Lou and me go there with you? We could stay quiet in the grounds or kitchens."

"Could I come too?" Tom asked.

Dick said nothing. He had come in late from Claremont and ate silently.

Mr. Edsir looked both alarmed and angry. "Certainly not. The Duke wouldn't want children there, especially with the King coming."

"No, indeed," his wife agreed and I thought there was a special secret look between them.

"The Palace isn't what it was, alas," Mr. Edsir went on. "So many of the Gentry have apartments there, servants quarrelling, little dogs yapping and misbehaving, their cooks causing confusion in the kitchens. Only the King's quarters and the Great Hall are left in peace."

Bet slipped into my room that night with a book. "It's a

Romance," she explained. "Lady Susan left it in the school-room and I borrowed it. You could help me, Lou, with the difficult words."

"You'll have to take it back," I said.

"Tomorrow. I promise."

We took turns to read out loud. Bet grew excited by the story but I found my concentration wandering, first to my encounter with the Captain, which was much more romantic than this silly story.

Then I wondered why the Edsirs had always been reluctant to take us to Hampton Court, even to the more lowly Servants' Hall. Papa Edsir had always described the Palace as "summat amazing – takes your breath away." But we'd never been allowed to go with him.

Was there some secret in that great Palace which would lead me to find out more about my parents?

CHAPTER 9

The following day, Miss Wildbore was showing us places on the Globe and telling us about the Penal Colony in New South Wales, the other side of the world. "King George has claimed the land for Britain," she said. "But I've heard that there are savages there who resent white men and kill them."

"But isn't it the savages' land first, Miss?" Bet asked. "I'd fight if our village was invaded by anyone, specially criminals."

Miss Wildbore began to lecture her and under cover of all the talk, Susan whispered, "Louisa, you certainly chose a handsome rescuer when you fell off!"

I bent over my books to hide the give-away blush.

Miss Wildbore was frowning at them but Susan went on, "I wonder if he'll come this way again."

I whispered back, "I doubt it. He's going off to Ireland with his Regiment." I felt a pang of regret as I said it.

At last Miss Wildbore said we would go outside to sketch.

The little black boy, Samuel, and a footman followed them, carrying stools and easels. I smiled at the boy and he grinned back, showing perfect white teeth against his black skin. He moved back on Susan's orders to wait with the footman while we drew.

I felt sorry for him. "He can't be more than ten years old, Lady Susan. Isn't he too young to be away from home, wherever that is?"

Susan frowned. "I don't think of him as a child. My grand-father gave him to me and I am training him to work his way up in our household. I believe his parents came from Africa but are now dead." Her voice sharpened. "I can assure you, he is as well treated as the rest of our servants. One day he may become a footman."

Africa – I had heard of the slave trade, bringing blacks from beautiful jungles to work for white men in England and America, where the trade still went on. I'd read in the Reverend's newspapers of the arguments against slavery and I hoped Samuel would one day be a free man. I looked back and smiled at him. He had lost his mother, like me.

Samuel gave me a broad smile, his teeth white against his dark skin.

The Tyrconnells had given me a box of water-colours at Christmas and I now shared these with Bet. I wondered how to portray the lake, with its wonderful reflections of the golds and reds of the autumn leaves.

Miss Wildbore was doing a careful sketch while impatient Susan splashed colours on damp paper so they ran together. The result was messy but somehow caught the spirit of the place.

Bet was reproved for ignoring the scene but drawing exaggerated likenesses of them all, including Miss Wildbore, whose long nose poked mournfully out of her bonnet. "Like a mouse," Bet whispered to me.

I wondered if the governess heard her because she said it was time to go back to the house, walking ahead of us and blowing her nose on a lace handkerchief. Susan looked at her stooped back. "I'd hate to be her, dependant on a family like us for everything." I liked Susan better for showing some feeling but she was sharp, ordering the footman and Samuel to carry everything back. "We'll go a different way," she said and led us past a Grotto and a strange-looking tower, the Belvedere that Bet had mentioned.

"Is that where you keep a mad old aunt, Lady Susan?" Bet asked.

"Just call me Susan, please." She laughed. "No mad old aunts but the gentlemen sometimes play cards there. Come on, girls, I have a longing for cold lemonade."

In the old nursery, next to the schoolroom, a maid brought tiny pies, cakes, ripe peaches and apricots from the Conservatory and a tall jug of lemonade. We ate off fine china and used silver knives and forks. Miss Wildbore gave a short lecture on the use of cutlery at a dinner-party.

Bet giggled. "I can't see myself at dinner-parties! I'm likely to be a spinster schoolteacher. Besides, I would die of boredom trying to ape the Gentry."

I held my breath, feeling she had gone too far but Susan was silent a moment, then said, "I almost envy you, Elizabeth. My parents are already encouraging a doddery old Earl who favours me. He must be as old as fifty and covers his balding head with a huge old-fashioned wig. And he has hairs sprouting from his nostrils and ears!"

Miss Wildbore looked disapproving as she cut her peach into neat segments with a tiny silver knife. "Lady Susan – I really do not think you should criticise your parents, especially in front of Louisa and Elizabeth."

We were back in the school-room, copying out a Psalm, when the maid came in and said Lady Tyrconnell wished to speak to Miss Wildbore, who left the room, spots of colour on her mottled cheeks. I guessed she lived in fear of displeasing the Tyrconnells and losing her post.

"I hate copying out poems and Psalms – it's so boring!" Susan took off her frilly cap and undid the pins from her mass of hair. "A plague on my parents!" she said. "I hardly see them. My Mama is here today but she often takes to her bed with her cough or she is off with her Royal lover now he is back from Holland. Perhaps he will lose interest in her now she has become ill. And my Papa is often away in London or Scotland now he's a Member of Parliament."

Miss Wildbore came back. "Her Ladyship wishes to see

your paintings and also to hear how Susan's music is progressing. I may say, girls, Lady Susan plays Mozart very well. So, Louisa and Elizabeth, what would you like to sing?"

"I sing like a croaking frog," Bet said cheerfully. "I'd rather look at that book on birds and animals."

I felt nervous. "I've only played a little Bach and accompanied myself singing songs and hymns."

"That will be quite enough, dear," Miss Wildbore said.

We went down to Red Withdrawing-Room, so called, Susan said, because of the dark red walls and red-patterned Persian carpet. A harpsichord stood at one end, facing a row of chairs.

Lady Tyrconnell swept in with a rustle of her elegant silk gown, her beautiful face very pale. She sank into a chair while Susan attacked the instrument with her usual vigour. At the end, Susan stood up and did a little curtsey and we all clapped.

"Is that a new piece, Susan?" her mother asked.

"No, Mama. It's some time since you heard me play." Her voice was both angry and reproachful.

Her mother looked sad and coughed delicately into a lace handkerchief.

"Now, your turn, Louisa," Susan ordered me.

My fingers trembled as I played but I knew the familiar Bach fugue by heart. The harpsichord was a better one than at the Rectory and I stopped feeling self-conscious as I went on to accompany myself playing a hymn and then a song. I finished by singing a cheerful Christmas carol.

The clapping surprised me and Lady Tyrconnell said, "You have a remarkable and true voice, Louisa."

I curtsied and mumbled my thanks, feeling overcome. I had only ever played for the Rector and his wife.

Lady Tyrconnell actually smiled at me. "We are giving a dinner-party next week – I wonder if you would play and sing for us afterwards. Susan will play her piece too."

"I don't know..." I stammered.

"The honour has overwhelmed her, My Lady," Miss Wildbore said quickly.

That was almost true. I was excited and yet nervous. I had sung at the Maying ceremony and in church but I'd never given a performance before.

I saw Bet, looking up from her book with a sour expression. I had to include her, somehow.

"I will try my best, your Ladyship," I said politely. "I have sheet music at home. I need someone to turn the pages." This wasn't really true and Bet couldn't read music. "Could my sister Elizabeth accompany me?"

Bet was smiling now and nodding and she didn't notice Lady Tyrconnell's small gasp of surprise, before she said, "Perhaps Elizabeth might come as a chaperone."

Bet jumped up, all smiles. "Yes, please, My Lady!"

Lady Tyrconnell began to cough and had to ring for her maid, who brought some healing syrup. Then Miss Wildbore helped her leave the room.

When we were on our own, I began to panic. "What should I wear? I've nothing suitable."

"Our seamstress will make you a dress," Susan said. "I shall ask her to come tomorrow, bringing lengths of silk. What colour would you choose? How about a midnight blue, with small sprigs of white flowers? She brought that last time. Or with your hair – a blue shot with green – like a Kingfisher."

I pictured the kingfisher I'd seen, flashing down the river. "Yes, thank you, I should like that. And what about Bet?"

"At her age, a simple white silk or muslin might be best. I am wearing a cream silk dress, shot with tiny rays of gold."

"Maybe I could have a bright blue sash?" Bet asked hope-fully.

"Perhaps." Susan looked at me. "Be careful some old nobleman doesn't whisk you away, Louisa!"

"Our Lou has no money, no dowry to offer and my brother Dick told me he has hopes…" Bet said.

"Your foster-brother?" Susan asked, looking surprised.

67

I wanted to run away and hide. Then I was angry with Bet for telling family secrets to Susan. "Bet! Lady Susan won't be interested in my marriage prospects." My voice was cold and Bet scowled at me.

Miss Wildbore came back with a bunch of flowers she had begged from one of the gardeners and set us to draw and make notes until the time came for us to go home.

Susan came to the stables with us and smiled at Dick, who was patiently waiting with Billy and the dog-cart.

"Your brother is so good-looking," she whispered. "If only he had a title and lands I'd be after him!" She linked arms with us. "I'm so glad you're coming here each day. This place is dull after London and my grandfather Delaval's home in Yorkshire. Did you know his house is full of tricks we play on guests? There's a device hidden in the walls of the guest rooms, so when the happy couple are half-naked or otherwise engaged…" she giggled, "a lever is pushed and the wall slides apart so everyone can see them." She winked suggestively. "And some of the beds are suspended over trap-doors so when the guests retire, they are let down into a cold bath, or you can fall asleep in a room which turns around, so when you wake, the tables and chairs are stuck to the ceiling and the chandelier is in the middle of the floor!"

We laughed politely but I thought it all sounded rather childish and I wondered if anyone ever came back to stay at the Hall.

As Dick drove us back through the village, Martha's husband, Jed, ran from the cottage next to the forge, where a bay horse was tethered for shoeing. "Dick – tell your mother Martha's baby is on its way but she's in sore pain."

"We'll stop here and help with the little ones," I said.

"Oh, poor Martha!" Bet had grown pale.

Dick looked worried. "Give Martha my best love and I hope the baby will arrive safely. I'll go on and tell Ma, then return."

"Mistress Thorogoode is with her," Jed told us, his round

68

face creased with worry. "She's tried all her remedies. And I have to shoe this horse for a gentleman who is returning quite soon.

CHAPTER 10

I could hear Martha's groans as we went into the small thatched cottage. Upstairs, little Moses was screaming and trying to climb out of his wooden cradle and his sister, Mary, was hitting at the closed door to her mother's room with tiny fists, yelling "Maa!" and sounding like a lost lamb. She had wet herself and stood in a pool of piss.

Mistress Thorogoode, village midwife and brewer of herbs – and some said, of spells – rushed into the room, bringing a smell of blood and her musky herbal medicines.

"Bet and Lou – your sister's taken bad this time," she panted. The others came so sweet and easy. Even with my poppy-seed potion she's in great pain and yet the baby doesn't come. Both will die if we cannot help her. She needs a Surgeon."

Bet's face was white. "We have to see her!"

"You can't help. Best mind the babies." Mistress Thorogoode went back to Martha, shutting the door firmly behind her.

Bet was trying not to cry. "I want to see our Martha," she repeated.

I felt shaken but we had to obey the midwife. "Bet – we're best doing what she says."

For once, Bet didn't argue. She changed Mary's shift and found her wooden doll, then went for the water. I changed Moses' soaked clouts and gown and fed him with pap – mixing bread, milk and water. His shawl was soaked so I wrapped him tight in mine and rocked him to sleep. I felt a strange love and longing as I looked down at the baby, seeing the long black lashes against his small rosy cheek and his doll-sized thumb in his mouth. One day I wanted a baby like Moses.

I stood up, feeling dizzy, and for a strange moment I had a strange vision of myself surrounded by my children, a baby in my arms. But who was to be the father?

Then Mistress Thorogoode called us in.

The room on this warm day was stifling. I went to open the window but the old midwife told me not to. "Letting the evil air in like that!" she scolded.

Martha's white face was running with sweat as she tried to smile at us and clutched at our hands. "This one doesn't want to see the world." Her voice was weak.

The midwife looked anxious as she wiped Martha's face. "The baby's lying feet first. I've given Martha a potion to make her push and one to dull the pain. My very best herbs. But she's growing so weak…"

She didn't finish.

Outside, the world went on normally. I heard the hiss of a hot horse-shoe fitted to a hoof, the pedlar calling his wares and the rumbling of the mail coach as it thundered on its way to London.

I drew Bet to the window. "We have to get the Surgeon for her."

Bet shook her head. "Lou – you know old Dr. Cutlack does nothing but bleed his patients and he's often drunk. Remember – he was useless when Tom broke his arm falling from the stack. It's never set properly. They say Dr. Cutlack's buried more patients than cured them."

"Didn't Papa talk of a great Surgeon at Hampton Court?" I asked.

"Would he come here? And who will pay him?"

"I will," I said. "I've money saved from the Tyrconnells' gifts. We can use that. And Papa said he was going there today

71

so he can speak for us."

"But who will take the message? Dick has to go back to Claremont."

Mrs. Edsir burst into the room, red-faced and with a streak of flour on her face. "I was at the Mill when Dick came for me. Oh, my darling child. You look in great pain."

"I have tried all my skills, Mistress Edsir," said the old midwife. The child is ill-omened, lying feet-forward and will not be turned."

Mama Edsir clenched her hands as if to take Martha's pain. "If only Dr. Cutlack hadn't taken to the drink."

Suddenly I knew what to do. "We're going to drive to Hampton to fetch Dr. FitzAllen – one of the doctors Papa mentioned, who have been treating the King in his recent illness."

"He'll never come here!" Mama's voice was muffled as she bent over Martha. "And who'll fetch him?"

"We will," I said firmly. "Papa said he was at Hampton Court today – we can drive Billy there and find him so he can seek out the doctor."

"But you have never been there – do you know the way?"

"We can find it," Bet said above the noise baby Mary made banging on the door and crying. "Ma – in the meantime the little ones need you. We'll be as quick as we can."

We ran down the stairs. As we passed the forge, we saw Jed talking to a tall man holding the bay horse's reins. There was something familiar about him.

Dick was waiting outside with Billy and the trap. "How is she?" he asked anxiously

"She needs a Surgeon," I said. "We're going to Hampton Court if you can spare Billy."

"On your own? I could drive you," he said. "But I promised Carter I would be back to exercise the horses and get the carriage cleaned for Lord Tyrconnell's journey tomorrow. Carter's already annoyed that I'm taking so much time off to take you both to Claremont and back."

The man with Jed turned round and I saw he was the Captain. Despite my fears for Martha, I felt a strange jolt of happiness as he raised his hat. "Miss Louisa," he said. "What a chance meeting!"

Jed's face was full of anxiety. "Sir, excuse me a moment," he said to the Captain. "How is my Martha?" he asked them.

"Not good but Mama is with her and the babies. We are fetching Dr. FitzAllen from Hampton," I told him.

"Is someone ill?" the Captain asked.

"My wife is taken bad in childbirth."

"And we are going to find the Surgeon for my sister at Hampton Court," Bet added, with a gleam in her eye as she bobbed a curtsy.

The Captain looked concerned. "I'm so sorry to hear about your sister. You're right to get the best surgeon for her. Do you know the way to Hampton Court?"

"We'll follow the sign-posts, Sir." I remembered his pleasant deep voice so well but I also thought of my fall and how much he had seen of my legs and ankles, so I turned away, embarrassed, to unhitch Billy's reins from the post.

The Captain stared at us intently. "I'll be happy to lead the way and perhaps find the doctor for you. Your brother, Miss Louisa, has shod my horse well and I've time on my hands."

"We could not possibly trouble you, Sir," I said formally.

"I would be glad to be of service to you." He looked into my eyes again and for a moment, I couldn't look away.

Mrs. Edsir ran out. "She's asking for you, Jed. Normally so placid, tears ran down her face. "I fear for both mother and baby. We need the surgeon."

Bet hugged her. "We'll go at once, Ma."

"I shall lead the way," the Captain said, handing us up the step into the dog-cart. I found I was ridiculously comforted by his firm hand under my elbow but Dick was glaring at him.

As we drove off, I heard Dick's disapproving voice; "They

73

are going with a stranger, Ma."

It was hateful knowing Dick was angry but Martha mattered most.

The sun was hidden behind mustard-coloured clouds and the air felt heavy. I felt hot, the pins had fallen of my hair so my loose curls sprang out wildly, and my skirt was splodged with milk and worse, from the babies. Passing coaches smothered us with dust.

The Captain wouldn't think I was beautiful now. Then I told myself off sharply for being vain and even thinking of him when Martha was in such pain.

"How are we going to find this Surgeon?" Bet asked, flapping the reins on Billy's back to keep him up with the Captain's horse.

"I don't know but I hope we'll see Papa there and he'll know." I lowered my voice although with the noise of hooves, the Captain wasn't likely to hear me. "Bet – did you realise the Captain's the same soldier who helped me up yesterday when I fell off? And insisted on riding back with me?"

"I guessed that when he knew your name and the way you went red as a raspberry." Bet laughed. "Then I remembered he was the officer who threw back our shuttlecock."

I had been puzzling about something. "Isn't it strange that he should come to have his horse shod in our village? And that his horse should lose a shoe so soon after we met? I would have thought there was an Army farrier at the barracks."

"Not so strange, Lou! He was very probably thinking of paying you a visit."

I smiled but my heart beat fast. "Don't be so ridiculous! Why would an Army Captain seek out a farmer's daughter?"

"Foster-daughter," Bet reminded her. "And his intentions may not be honourable, Lou. Take care."

"It's most unlikely that I shall ever see him again," I said decisively. "Bet – move over and let me take the reins now. I can hear a coach approaching and you know Billy might shy."

74

Bet muttered, "I can manage old Billy. It's just because you want to show off to the Captain."

I didn't answer because my thoughts had switched back to poor Martha. Would they get the Surgeon in time and was he likely to come? Would the Captain help us if we couldn't find Papa?

I looked ahead at the Captain's broad shoulders and the way he sat so easily on his horse and felt a strange pang. Then I told myself not to be a hopeless romantic, like the heroines of Bet's Romances. Life just wasn't like that.

And I had hoped to visit the Palace one day to see if I could untangle the secret of my birth. Today, though, there would be no time to find out anything.

The sky grew darker and there was a roll of thunder. Then rain began to splatter down. Soon we were soaked and could hardly see the road ahead nor the sign-posts.

After what seemed an age, a lightening flash illuminated the gates to the Palace and the huge red-brick building ahead. A uniformed man carrying a large umbrella stopped us and the Captain bent to speak to him.

"He might not let us through," Bet said. "Didn't Pa say the King was coming here soon, on a short visit?"

The rain was trickling down my face and blurring my eyelashes so I could hardly see what was going on and I wished I'd not left my bonnet at Martha's.

There seemed to be a short argument but at last, two men opened the gates and we drove up to the imposing Palace with its many towers, massive gateway, and the Royal flag flying.

We stopped in front of the building, a few paces from a gleaming carriage bearing a Royal Coat of Arms and drawn by four perfectly matched black horses. Just as the Captain dismounted, two footmen came out, holding a big umbrella over an important-looking man, dressed in the latest fashion.

As he approached his coach, a flash of lightning illuminated the scene and I saw him looking at us and frowning. He had a large nose, bulging eyes and full lips. I didn't like the look of him at all and hoped he wasn't the King. A footman helped him into his carriage.

Two guards ran up to us. "You should go to the servants' entrance," the largest one said in a furious voice. "Please move at once."

The Captain gave the reins of his horse to a boy and walked up to them. "These ladies are under my protection," he said. I'm Captain Godfrey Macdonald and we seek the Surgeon, Mr. FitzAllen, for a very important person."

The leading guard saluted. "Sir! His Royal Highness the Duke of Gloucester has been visiting Hampton Court. You may speak to his Steward."

So that was the Duke, the King's brother and our Papa's employer. I decided I wouldn't want to work for him.

"Pa!" Bet cried out as Mr. Edsir came out of the huge entrance, a boy leading his horse. At that moment, the Duke's outriders leaped on and the carriage drove off.

Mr. Edsir hurried up, frowning when he saw the dog-cart. Captain Macdonald touched his arm and spoke to him, then turned to speak to one of the guards. Flinging the reins at a young groom, he hurried inside the great archway.

Papa Edsir came up to us. "I hear our Martha is in trouble. You shouldn't be here. Why didn't our Dick come?"

"He had to go back to work," Bet interrupted. "Pa – we must find a doctor quickly."

"Have you sent for Dr Cutlack?"

I spoke urgently. "Dr. Cutlack's so often drunk and useless. Please help us find the Surgeon, FitzAllen, or Martha might die."

"But the expense…"

"I shall pay," I said with pride. I hoped the Tyrconnells' gifts of money I'd saved would be enough.

Mr. Edsir wiped his streaming face. "He might refuse. And why ask a stranger to bring you here? Is this your doing,

Louisa?" He was remembering my recent rebellion and I wanted to scream at him for wasting time.

Then I saw the Captain hurrying back. "Dr. FitzAllen will come," he said.

Mr. Edsir stared, lost for words for once.

Bet and I thanked the Captain. I found I was smiling at him, forgetting my dirty state. I was sure he smiled back at me. For a moment, I didn't care what his intentions might be – I only wanted to see him again.

"It was no trouble. I hope all goes well. Sir, Ladies," he bowed. "I am due back to Headquarters so I shall bid you goodbye." He remounted and was soon out of sight.

If only he had looked back.

It was a terrible evening. We looked after the babies and boiled up water on the kitchen fire while Dr. FitzAllen was with Martha. Then I drove Billy back to the farm through the sheeting rain to fetch my savings before Papa could object.

Still soaking wet and shivering I hurried back through the kitchen where Jed was pacing up and down while Mr. Edsir comforted himself with a flagon of cider. Dr. FitzAllen had looked appalled when he was led into the small cottage – obviously none of his patients were of such low status.

Mrs. Edsir came out of the bedroom, white-faced. "The Doctor is going to use an instrument to drag the poor baby out," she said. "And he has given my poor child laudanum to deaden the pain." Her voice broke. "He has warned us, she may not survive in this weakened state."

We both hugged her, encircled her with love to keep out the fear.

Young Moses slept through all the commotion but Bet was soon chasing after Mary, who yelled each time the thunder rolled and the rain battered the window.

At last, Martha gave a great cry and Mrs. Edsir ran into the room, shutting the door.

There was a dreadful silence.

Then Mrs. Edsir came out, with a tiny baby wrapped in a piece of bloody cloth. "She's not breathing! And the doctor and midwife are too busy with my poor Martha to look at the baby."

I remembered a lamb being born, unable to breathe. Our brother, Will, had a small flock of sheep in one of Papa's fields and this last spring we went there to help with the lambing.

Just as we arrived, a sheep gave birth to a lamb, which lay flat and dead-looking and did not revive when the mother licked it. Then Will put a finger in the lamb's mouth to clear its airway, then lifted it up by its back legs and waved it in the air until it gave a gasp and a bleat.

I turned to Bet. "Remember Will's lamb? Let me have her, Mama."

I took the blood-streaked baby from Mrs. Edsir's arms, gently putting my little finger in the tiny mouth. Fluid gushed out but still the baby didn't take a breath.

I almost panicked but made myself grasp the baby's slippery feet, scared out of my wits that I might drop her. I swung her gently, all the while stroking her tiny back with my free hand.

Mrs. Edsir's voice was hysterical. "Give me the baby, Louisa. Let her rest in peace."

The baby gasped and then cried out, thin and high as a kitten.

CHAPTER 11

"Now you have a baby named after you, Lou," Bet said as we walked on an errand to the Mill. "So you really are part of our family. You don't need to go on wondering if you are some poor relation of the Tyrconnells."

I smiled. Baby Louisa was thriving well and Martha had been strong enough to hold her at the Christening last week, surrounded by her six brothers and sisters, filling the church with babble and noise.

"A Godmother, too. And Ma didn't mind your lending the baby your very own shawl," Bet went on. "It looked so fine at the Christening."

In fact, I had to plead for the exquisite lacy shawl to be used. "After all, it is mine, Mama," I had said. "Even if you refuse to tell me about my mother."

A year ago, I would never have spoken to her like that but I'd found a new strength lately.

This afternoon, we were fetching flour from the Mill, ground from our own barley. It was a pleasant walk in the late afternoon sunshine, crunching through the fallen leaves and hearing the squirrels chatter above. There was a faint smell of smoke from the village bonfires and the river Mole glittered ahead, through the trees.

Chestnut leaves fluttered down and Bet jumped and caught one. "A year's good fortune!" she said. "I shall take it as an omen for my future as a schoolmistress. If only I was a man and could study at Oxford. It's not fair that women aren't allowed there."

I looked at her eager face. "I believe if you had lived in France, Bet, you'd be a Revolutionary."

Bet laughed. "Very likely. Who needs rich old Kings and Queens when people are starving?" She stooped to pick up a gleaming horse-chestnut. "I shall give this to Tom so he can have a conker-fight." She chattered on in her usual way, "You know what, Lou? Men think we have much smaller brains and they like to keep us in our place, minding them and having a baby each year."

I wished I didn't have to tell her but I said, "Bet, you remember when Lady Tyrconnell sent for me yesterday – while you were with the Seamstress, trying on your dress?"

"Yes. So what did Lady T. want?"

"She asked me if I would attend the dinner tomorrow myself, before I try to entertain her guests." I felt a nervous tingling. "Tell you the truth, Bet, I'm scared! I told her Ladyship I would like you to come too. She had one of her coughing fits so I didn't get an answer and I haven't seen her since."

Bet turned, and made a face. "You go alone. For all our lessons on becoming a Young Lady I would never remember which knife to use and as for talking to those po-faced Gentry, it's not for me. And don't you dare smile prettily at one of the Nobility. I want to keep you at the farm."

I gave her a hug. "Dick thinks the Tyrconnells are trying to groom me for marriage, although my lack of a dowry will put off any suitors. I've told you often, Bet, I don't want to marry for a long time." I linked my arm in hers. "And I love being with our family, even when Pa has one of his tempers."

I remembered Dick's words a few days ago, when I told him I was nervous of performing at Claremont. He had put his sun-burnt hand over mine. "You don't belong there, our Lou, do you? They tinker with your life without telling you the truth. And I reckon they hope to find a husband for you – by making you talk and behave like them. There's a guilty secret in that family, for sure, that's why they treat you so."

His hand was comforting and I felt a great fondness for him. I felt as if I were being pulled between two worlds – one familiar and the other threatening and almost artificial, where appearances seemed to matter so much.

Today, walking through the thickly fallen leaves, I felt I was looking at myself from outside. Who was I and what did I want? I had a fleeting memory of the Captain and the way he'd looked at me.

Bet read my mind. "Do you ever think of that handsome soldier who came to the forge – probably hoping to see you – and then helped us find the doctor? And you told me he had already paid the Surgeon."

I laughed. "I'm mortified to remember the time he rescued me and saw my skirts fly over my head! I am so grateful for his help and his money but I've put him from my mind. He said he was going to Ireland."

I hadn't forgotten him and had hoped he might ride our way again. "I think you were wrong," I went on. "He wasn't trying to find me when he came to Jed's forge. It was just a coincidence. Besides, what a sight we must have been that day – I saw myself later in Mama's looking-glass and my face was streaked with rain and dust."

We came to the river. The watermill churned and its ripples broke up the colours of the reflected trees into beautiful patterns. I wished I could capture the scene in a painting.

"You're probably right, Lou," Bet said. "I expect the Captain is engaged to a rich and high-born girl. Now, what about Dick? You know he's sweet on you and you've always been so fond of him."

"I am – but…"

Bet interrupted me, "Be careful, Lou, you don't lose our Dick. If you turn into a Young Lady he'll find someone else.

You know our dairymaid, Daisy, is sweet on him? And when she's washed the smell of cows off her and dresses for Sunday, he looks at her. She's a pretty girl, strong and willing and would make a good wife."

I did not answer and we walked on in silence.

On the way back we were burdened with heavy sacks of flour and I noticed Bet was walking slowly. "Are you feeling all right?" I asked her.

She rubbed drops of perspiration off her hot face, although the autumn air was crisp. "It's nothing. I've a cold coming. A headache – and my throat is sore. A dose of Ma's Hartshorne remedy should put me right."

I insisted on carrying her bag as well as my own. I felt a stab of fear. There was fever going round the village and I remembered when the smallpox came, only a few years ago. Our family had escaped but others had not.

When we arrived home, Bet refused supper and went to bed. Mama brought her a posset and her evil-smelling Hartshorne medicine.

I put a cold wet cloth on Bet's brow and read out loud from Susan's Romance, which she'd said Bet could keep. At last Bet fell into a feverish sleep and Mama told me to go to bed.

I couldn't sleep at first but when I did I dreamed I was at a funeral, walking behind the black plumed horses and I knew they were pulling the hearse containing Bet's body. Then the coffin lay in church, open but Bet wasn't there and I knew that the woman lying there was my mother.

Waking with a jolt, tears running down my face, I pulled Tobias onto my bed and held his shaggy body close.

I heard the cock crow outside but it was still very early when I crept into Bet's room. In the pale first light my sister was awake, tossing in the bed, sweat pouring down her face.

"Don't look so worried, Lou," Bet croaked. "Tis only a touch of fever. But I do feel like I am on fire. Yesterday by the river, I was so hot I wished I could jump into the water."

I opened the small window and fetched water from the kitchen.

"It's fresh and cool," I told her. "Tom pumped it up from the well yesterday." I took off her sweat-soaked nightgown and dipped a cloth in the water, gently washing down my sister's skinny body. As yet, there was no tell-tale rash.

"Oh Lou – that feels better," Bet murmured.

Mama hurried into the room. "Whatever are you doing, Louisa? The child will die of cold lying there with the window open." She started to pull the quilt over Bet but I put out my hand.

"Don't! We need to bring her fever down. Remember how it worked, that time Tom caught the scarlet fever."

Mama put her hand on Bet's forehead. "I pray it's only a fever. I wish we could afford that Dr. FitzAllen again. But I suppose Dr. Cutlack might help if he's sober."

Bet whispered, "Ma – don't send for Dr. Cutlack. Even if he's not in his cups, he'll want to bleed me – that's the only cure he knows."

Her mother brought out a bottle and spoon from her apron. "This will cure you for sure, the Mixture – Hartshorne, honey, Feverfew and my secret herb. It's cured all you children of fever." She paused. "Except my little Richard." She sighed. "And Louisa, you shouldn't be in here. You are going to that grand dinner today."

"I won't go if Bet's so sick." I couldn't bear to leave her.

Bet reached up and clutched my arm. "You must go, Lou. You have practised so hard each day. I'll refuse Ma's medicine otherwise."

"I'll wait and see how you are first," I promised.

Papa prayed for Bet's recovery when he said Grace at breakfast. Then he said, "I hear, Louisa, you want to nurse your sister." His dark eyes softened, for once. "That's very kindly meant but you're expected at Claremont today. And you can't refuse the honour of playing and singing in front of such a company of Gentry." He cleared his throat as if embarrassed. "You are now a young lady of nearly seventeen and it be our duty to think of your future."

"Duty?" I asked. I wanted love, not duty.

Mama darted a look at her husband. He added, with an effort, "And of course we regard you almost as one of our own."

"Almost." There it was again, not really belonging. And what was my future?

I ran upstairs to see how Bet fared. She was asleep, sucking her thumb like a child and I fancied a little less flushed.

I made Mama promise not fetch Dr. Cutlack and said I'd go to Claremont.

Dick was silent as he drove me there, through lanes whose hedges were decorated with fluffy Old Man's Beard and honeysuckle berries, glowing like drops of blood in the sunlight. It was the kind of day I usually loved, but not now, with Bet so ill. How could I forget Bet's sickness while I practised my music, ready for the ordeal of the dinner and worse, of my recital?

Dick was to drive me back late and he was to be given food. "I wish you didn't have to eat in the Servants Hall tonight while I'm being served a grand dinner," I said.

"Why not?" His voice was sharp. "I am a servant and the food will be good."

I clenched my hands to stop their trembling. "I wish I could have stayed with Bet."

He turned round and smiled at me. "Lou – please don't fret. Our Bet is strong and will recover. Our family is sturdy – all seven of us alive except for Richard. I took his name but I never gained Ma's heart because she was caught up in her grief."

I went to squeeze beside him on the driver's high seat. I'd

84

never before realised he had missed out on his mother's love. "They both love you. That time when Will complained you could be helping him on the farm, Pa said he was pleased you had ambition to be a coachman."

"Pa's so changeable. One minute shouting, the next friendly," he complained.

"I think he finds it a strain, trying to please as the Duke's steward and managing the farm. I saw the Duke, you know and he looks to be a demanding and perhaps difficult person, not likeable."

"You are right. And often Pa is kind in his way, even though you have crossed him lately." He turned and smiled. Suddenly the day grew brighter.

We were just passing the Quaker Meeting House in Claremont Lane when a horse appeared, trotting fast and raising a cloud of dust.

"Good morrow, Miss Louisa," and the Captain raised his hat.

I couldn't help smiling and I hardly had time to raise my hand before horse and rider had gone past. Dick was scowling. "Pa would be angry if he saw you waving at a gentleman like that," he said.

I tried to speak evenly and hide my delight. "Have you forgotten that the Captain helped us find a doctor for Martha?"

"I suspect his motives," Dick said darkly. "He has been abroad, fighting. Now he wants to seduce a pretty farm-girl."

I was suddenly angry. "Dick! How can you say such a thing? I am sure it is just coincidence – after all, he's quartered in Surrey. Perhaps he came to see the Tyrconnells."

"I hope they gave him short shrift."

Dick wished me well when we arrived and he helped me down but I felt we were growing apart. I didn't like it.

Susan said she was sorry to hear about Bet's illness but I could see she was totally taken up with her new dress and thoughts about the dinner-party.

"Did you have a visit from that Army Captain who helped me when Folly bolted?" I asked, when Susan stopped to take breath.

She smiled. "He asked for me and I did see him. I found him good company and changed my opinion of him and wish we could invite him here but of course, we know nothing of his background. I told him you were coming here to sing and play. He asked if you went each Sunday to church at Esher and I told him yes and you would soon be Confirmed. I also told him you were to sit next to Lord Archibald Malham, heir to the Earl of Bilsborough and that my Mama was bent on match-making. Then my Mama appeared, rigid with disapproval at my being with a stranger, unchaperoned, so he apologised for intruding and went off."

I was amazed she had talked to him. "So you told him a great deal about me." I wasn't sure what I felt – whether it pleased me or not.

Susan smiled. "He was so charming and handsome – I found myself chattering away…"

"In your usual style!"

"True. But I am a great asset at a dinner-party." She preened herself in front of her long cheval looking-glass. "Tonight I have to freeze off the Earl, even if it sends my Mama into a coughing fit."

I smiled but I was thinking of Dick's words of warning. Perhaps the Captain was trying to find out more about me but with what purpose? Obviously, he would now give up ideas of seduction, knowing the Tyrconnells had a suitor for me, a man of much higher rank. I greatly disliked the idea I was being shown off tonight, like a piece of goods.

Then I became absorbed in practising my music and songs, this time on the beautiful harpsichord in the large withdrawing-room. Chairs were already arranged for the guests and my fingers quivered with nerves as I touched the keys.

After I'd finished, Susan played her piece, then grew bored

and hurried me upstairs to her ornate bedroom, where everything seemed decorated with roses, the wallpaper and the
hangings round her four-poster bed and
curtains framing the big window.

We bathed in the warm rose-scented water, brought by the
maid to the ornate bathroom. I delighted in this treat – rather
different, I thought from the tin bath in front of the kitchen
fire.

Susan sprayed us both with rose perfume, sent from London
and her maid helped us dress, Susan in a cream silk gown,
threaded with gold, and a wide gold sash high under her full
breasts. Her shining hair was piled up in curls, the maid
letting some tendrils fall to frame her face. "Don't put on those
stupid stays," she told me. "They're so old-fashioned."

"I've always hated them," I said. "And you look wonderful.
If you are planning to discourage your Earl, it won't work!"

Susan looked at me carefully and I waited for criticism. It
didn't come. "May I return the compliment, Louisa? I shall
be quite jealous when I see the men stare at you!"

The maid finished my hair and I turned to stare into the long
looking-glass. I had been told that modern fashion favoured
muted colours or white but Susan had ordered the seamstress
to find a delicate green silk, shot with a blue. I had to admit,
it flattered me.

Susan was staring at me. "You know, now I look carefully
at you, our features are much alike."

"Yes – it's true," I admitted.

"Perhaps we're distantly related. Good! I've always wanted
a sister," and Susan gave me a quick kiss, light as a feather.

It felt strange and somehow wrong to let the maid put on
my silk stockings and embroidered garters – why were the
Gentry so helpless? My feet looked small and dainty in the
flower-embroidered silk slippers and they felt so light, after
wearing leather boots or wooden patterns round the farm.

"Now you must wear one of my necklaces."

I tried to protest but Susan insisted on my wearing a necklace of emeralds and deep blue sapphires, set in gold. I couldn't resist looking again into the mirror and felt the reflection was almost of a stranger, and a girl of at least eighteen.

Susan smiled. "Seeing you so pretty, some gentleman may well forget that you have no dowry. I can hear the carriages arriving. Come downstairs with me."

I was suddenly rigid with nerves. "I don't think I can move."

"Of course you can, silly!" She took my hand.

We walked down the grand staircase towards the bright hall, lit by a myriad candles in the glittering chandeliers.

CHAPTER 12

"Are you and Lady Susan related, Miss La Coast?" asked the man sitting next to me. "When you smile, you look alike."

The dinner was almost over, guests lingering over sweet-meats, jellies and fruit tarts, presided over by a large swan, carved of ice. I had never seen such a thing – Susan had told me that there was an ice-house, dug deep in the grounds. The swan was an improvement on the pig's head, which had appeared earlier and made me feel sick as I thought about my dear Bertha. The young pig lived outside now, with the cattle and sheep and came trotting, tail curled up, when I called her.

I was sitting between Lord Archibald Malham, who looked at least forty years old, and Susan's Earl. It was a relief that this balding man made only polite remarks to me before turning to Susan with a flow of compliments.

I felt bewildered by the grandeur of it all, the important-looking guests, dressed in the latest fashions, the gleaming silver and the footmen lining the walls of the huge Hall.

Perhaps the servants as well as the guests were looking down on me, a farm girl pretending to be a Young Lady. I thought of something Bet had said, "It don't matter that you can't name your parents – nor that we live on a farm. When you sing to those snobs, remember we're as good as them. Naked – you wouldn't tell the difference. They're born and die like us and like us, turn into bones and dust." I smiled at the memory of her typically blunt words.

"Did you hear me, Miss La Coast?" asked Lord Malham. "Is Lady Susan a cousin, perhaps?" He gave me a full-lipped smile and his dark eyes stared into mine so hard I had to look down.

At least he, unlike Susan's Earl, had a head of curly black hair and he wore the latest fashion. I had to admit, he was good-looking, and he had been attentive, helping me to various dishes and trying to entertain me with amusing little stories, mainly about himself. "There may be a distant connection, Sir," I admitted.

He lowered his voice, "You are the prettiest girl here, even more lovely than Lady Susan." I thought I felt his silk-clad calf press against my dress under the table and I tried to move a little away. "I believe you are to entertain us shortly?" he asked.

"Yes – my Lord." I spoke formally, hoping to put him off..

This time he put his hand over mine in my lap. "You are trembling, Miss La Coast. There is no need to be nervous. Whatever you play, everyone will be looking at your lovely face."

I was trembling with anger at his presumption but before I could say anything, I saw Lady Tyrconnell getting up and the other ladies following her. Susan told me the ladies went to the withdrawing-room and left the men to their drinking and telling of bawdy stories. "You will have time to recollect yourself before you play," she had added.

It was good to get away from his overpowering presence. "I have to go, Sir," I said, getting up.

He stood too, bowing. "I look forward to your performance, Miss La Coast."

I gathered up my dress and ran upstairs, past the withdrawing-room and up to the grand water-closet near Susan's room, where I was sick. I wasn't used to rich food and wine and I was scared witless about playing to such a throng.

Susan found me, gave me water and put rouge on my pale cheeks. Then she brought me back to the Red Room. "Just play for me before they come," she said. "The ladies will be a little while, gossiping and sipping tea."

I sat at the harpsichord and flexed my cold fingers. At first, they stumbled but soon I was playing my favourite Bach fugue and forgetting my fears.

The ladies came in first, then the gentlemen.

Susan was to play first, so I sat on a small gilded chair beside the harpsichord.

Miss Wildbore arrived, having been banished to the nursery for her supper. She wore an old-fashioned dull grey dress, only relieved by a little white lace on top of the bodice. Her face was a mottled red, as if she hated to be on show, as she arranged the music for Susan, who curtsied, and went to play her piece without much feeling.

Her parents led the clapping, and her old grandfather, Lord Duval called, "Bravo!"

Lady Tyrconnell got up, coughing as usual, but managed to announce that Miss La Coast would play and sing for them. I had pleaded to be called Edsir but nobody listened.

The Bach fugue went well. Then I accompanied myself, playing simple country songs and finishing with Green-sleeves.

Everyone clapped and someone called, "Bravo!" I curtsied and tried to hurry off but everyone applauded even more and Lord Malham asked if I could sing just one more song. "Your voice is as pure as a nightingale's," he gushed. I felt like throwing the music at him and would have refused but Susan came forward and whispered,

"Just one more, please, Louisa."

I looked above the heads of my audience at the glittering chandeliers and sang an old song, one of Bet's favourites because it praised ordinary folk.

On the brow of the hill a young shepherdess dwelt,
who no pangs of ambition or love had e'er felt.
For a few further maxims still ran in her head

91

that twas better to earn, ere she eat her brown bread:
That to rise with the lark was conducive to health
and to folks in a cottage contentment was wealth.

Then I curtsied and made my way past the guests, hurrying out of a far door and into a long corridor. I heard footsteps behind me and quickened my pace but Lord Malham's voice followed me. "I hope you aren't leaving us, Miss Louisa."

His hand was now on my bare arm. I tried to shake it off but his grip tightened. "Your voice is as lovely as you, Miss La Coast." He was so close I could smell cigar-smoke, wine and his male, sweaty self.

"Please leave me alone! I have to go home – my sister is ill." I spoke loudly and with anger but he didn't seem to be listening. He now put a strong arm round my waist and virtually pulled me through two more doors and into a big conservatory. "Please call me Archie," he murmured. "I just want to talk to you on our own."

I felt almost faint, with his strong smell blending with the scent of the plants in the huge conservatory, where lemons grew on small trees and huge palm trees reared up, surrounding us like a jungle, heated by a stove.

He almost pushed me to a carved bench. "Sit here a moment, please, my dear Louisa, where I can admire your lovely face."

The wine and the heat made me feel dizzy so I sat down, trying to leave a space between us and wondering if my reputation would suffer, being alone with him.

He moved nearer to me. "My fiancée died of typhoid fever last year." His voice was low and sad.

I had to say I was sorry but I still tried to move away.

He took my hand and held it in an iron grip. "I am an only son and my father, the Earl of Bilsborough, is failing," His voice was low, urgent. "He wants me to marry and give him an heir but I haven't met a girl I could love – until now."

I was shocked and trembling. What could I say? "Sir – I am only sixteen and a farmer's daughter with no dowry." That should put him off.

"I'm rich enough for both and I can soon make you forget your origins when you live in luxury," he persisted. His grip loosed so I wriggled out of his grasp, got up and made for the door. The tiny heel of my silk slipper caught on something and fell off but there was no time to pick it up as he was behind me, calling for me to stop.

I took off the other slipper and ran, twisting down corridors until his voice faded.

I had to find Dick.

CHAPTER 13

A lantern gleamed in the stable-yard and I found Dick slumped in the cart, half asleep, while Billy munched hay.

When he saw me he leaped out and stared at my feet, already dirty from the yard. "Why are you bare-foot? What's wrong?"

"A stupid accident – my heel broke off." I didn't like lying to him but I knew Dick's quick temper – if he knew the true story, he would have rushed in and attacked Archie Malham, not caring if he lost his position for assaulting an Earl's son.

"Did it go well?" he asked as he helped me into the dog-cart.

"Yes – my music was well received but the dinner..." I stopped.

"You felt out of place, I can tell." He urged Billy away from his hay and out of the yard. "You can't trust the Gentry. I have heard things about the King's own brothers. They have poor morals. You don't belong with the Gentry, Lou. Stay with us and be happy and free."

I looked back, and thought I saw the shadowy figure of a man coming after us. Carriages still lined the drive, ragged boys holding the waiting horses. I realised I had left without a word of thanks to Susan and her parents.

"You may be right," I said. "Dick – please hurry so we can see how Bet does."

Mama met us in the hall. Her hair was disordered and her face very pale. "She's still very bad," she said. "I fear the worst."

"I'll sit with her – you get some rest," I said.

I ran upstairs, not stopping to take off my fine dress and I spent the rest of the night sponging Bet's feverish body and trying to get her to drink a sup of milk and water. The thought of losing my sister made me cry and I prayed she would be saved. I spoke to her all the while but she didn't appear to hear – just tossed her head from one side to the other, each breath rasping in her throat.

There was a banging on the front door followed by voices in the hall. I woke and found I was half-lying against the bed. Morning light came through the thin curtain.

Bet lay very still.

I heard myself cry out as I bent over her, leaning close to that dead white face. Then I felt a gentle breath on my cheek.

She was alive and her forehead was cool.

Mrs Edsir rushed into the room. "Louisa! I've overslept!" She put her hand on Bet's forehead. "Dear Jesus! The fever has passed! Thank God!"

"She needs warm milk…"

"Yes – I will fetch it and sit with her but you need to tidy yourself and come downstairs. That beautiful dress is all creased and crumpled. Louisa – a titled gentleman has driven up in a grand coach and is talking with Mr.Edsir in the parlour. The gentleman says he met you last night and you lost a shoe. How could that be? He has brought flowers…" She found my silk shawl on the floor and put it round my shoulders. "He was obviously taken with you."

I couldn't believe it – I thought I had shown what I felt but Archie Malham had pursued me with my shoe. "I do not want to see him – especially like this."

"He looks a pleasant and well-dressed man." Mrs. Edsir was almost pushing me towards the door. "You could thank him for the shoe, at least. Though I cannot understand why you came home without it. And Bet needs warm milk, please."

I tidied my dress and put on my own worn slippers. I tried

to creep down to the kitchen but Tobias wuffed joyously when he saw me and Papa Edsir hurried after me, grabbing my arm.

He was red-faced but smiling. "Come into the parlour at once, Louisa. Lord Malham wishes to see you."

"I'm fetching milk for Bet – she's recovering."

"So I hear – God has spared her. But His Lordship has come specially to see you. He tells me he is the heir to the Earl of Bilsborough and they have a great estate. He realises you have no dowry to give a husband but he says it will be of no account and asked that he might court you. Of course, I agreed."

I felt I might explode with anger. "How could you, Papa! You didn't consult me and I refuse to consider him. And he's more than twice my age."

He still held my arm, so hard it hurt. "Louisa! You're being both rude and ungrateful. I have your best interests at heart. Do you want to be a poor spinster, living at home?" His voice softened. "I wouldn't force you to marry before you are eighteen but you could be betrothed. I understand you have only just met Lord Malham and I suppose you need to know him better."

"I shall marry for love, naught else," I said quietly. "It matters not at all to me if my husband be rich or poor, titled or a plain man. And I…"

He interrupted me. "Pigheaded child! You'll be sorry for these foolish ideas. And at least thank Lord Malham for returning your shoe."

Quickly, I decided I had to appear to obey. It was too late to escape. I let Papa take me into the parlour.

Archie Malham stood up and bowed when I came in and took a great bunch of bright autumn flowers and foliage from the footman, tied with a green silk ribbon.

He held them out, smiling and saying, "These flowers reminded me of you, Miss La Coast. And I have your shoe. I am very sorry you left so suddenly. I enjoyed our solitary tête-à-tête."

"You were alone together?" Mr. Edsir looked horrified.

"Miss La Coast insisted on showing me the Conservatory." His smile did not reach his eyes.

I stared back at him, defiantly. "I think your memory, Lord Malham, is misleading." I took the flowers and curtsied. "I thank you, Sir. Now I have to tend my sick sister."

Before he could reply, I left the room, shaken but determined. He might be rich and good-looking but there was a cold streak within him. I certainly would never want to be his wife.

I brought the warm milk to Bet and found her sitting up. "What happened? I heard voices, arguing," Bet asked.

I tried to make the encounter sound amusing.

Bet laughed until she coughed. "So – he wasn't Prince Charming!"

"What do you mean?"

"The Cinderella story – you left your shoe behind at midnight and he came to find the girl who wore it. Well, my feet are bigger than yours for all that I am younger. The slipper wouldn't fit this Ugly Sister!" She lay back, tired but smiling.

Papa radiated disapproval after this, as Archie Malham didn't give up. Over the next ten days, he sent letters, sealed with his crest, which I threw away. Then he sent a basket of fruit for "Your sick sister" and finally, a big pearl set in silver, hanging from an intricately worked silver chain. I found his address from Susan and sent it back by the Mail Coach before Papa Edsir could see it.

Susan laughed when she heard the story. "Well, you should be flattered, Louisa. He is titled and rich. And not as old as my Earl nor as hairy-nosed and bald. Should we swap?"

I laughed. "No thank you! He would be worse than Lord Malham!"

"Indeed," Susan agreed. "Anyway, I spoke to my admirer after the dinner and told him I loved another."

"Do you?" I asked in surprise.

97

She picked up a fan and hid her face behind it, giggling. "I have a secret love and I shall marry him one day, even if he doesn't know it yet. But you are fortunate your Papa didn't insist on your seeing Archie Malham. I did feel a little sorry for the poor man, since his fiancée has died but now he is telling lies about you I despise him." Her lively face looked serious, for once. "He could ruin your reputation with his lies. We couldn't think what had happened to you. Everyone wanted to congratulate you about your music. You quite over-shadowed me but I don't care! I'd rather ride than play music. Anyway, you must marry whom you love, like I shall."

I didn't remind her that her situation, with rich parents, was quite different. I had no dowry and I was really a penniless orphan, dependant on my foster-parents.

Mama Edsir tried more gently than Papa to persuade me to see Archie. "After all, dear child, you risked your reputation talking to him alone. I am afraid..."

I interrupted, "That he will tell the world I have a bad reputation? He dragged me into the conservatory against my will!"

Mama looked confused. "No – well, I just feel you should see him. It would do no harm to get acquainted. I fear Mr. Edsir might try to break down your opposition to the match. He feels responsible for your future."

"I would not want to toy with Lord Malham's affections." I was rather proud of this statement. It sounded grown-up and sensible, even if I had seen the expression in one of the Romances.

Dick, at least, was on my side when he heard the full story. "Pa's quite wrong. You only met this man once. And he's already told a lie – that you lured him into the conservatory. You cannot trust him, Lou."

As usual, I felt comforted by his support. He was so honest and plain spoken. I felt a sudden revulsion against the over-dressed Gentry with their false smiles.

As I fingered the miniature in my pocket, I wondered if I my mother had belonged to that set. I almost wished she had been a country girl, like myself – but that illusion was gone, now I had seen the expensive clothes she wore in the painting.

I still had to know the truth or I could never rest.

CHAPTER 14

By the day of the Confirmation, Bet was fully recovered.

Mama Edsir smiled at us. "You both look like angels in those white muslins."

"But you know better, Ma," Bet said with a cheeky grin.

The church was packed with villagers, all come to look at a real Bishop, dressed in his beautifully embroidered Cope and wearing his Mitre. Most of the Edsir family were there, except for Jed, who had work to do at the forge.

Lady Tyrconnell and Susan entered through their special doorway into their pew as the choir sang an anthem.

During the service, Bet and I joined the others being Confirmed, going up to the altar to be blessed by the Bishop.

After my Confirmation, I felt I was floating back down the aisle. I resolved to be good, even forgiving Papa Edsir for his harshness. I would work hard at my lessons, help more at home and visit the poor and elderly in the village. Then I faltered and almost stopped, holding up the procession.

The Captain was standing at the back of the church, looking directly at me and smiling. I found I was smiling back at him, amazed he was at the church.

"That's your gallant Captain," Bet whispered as we rejoined our parents for the final hymn and blessing. "Take care, Lou. Remember, you know nothing about him even if he did help us find the doctor."

Outside the church, a blustery autumn wind whipped at my dress and blew off my new lace-trimmed bonnet.

Then there he was again, coming up to me, holding the bonnet carefully, as if it were very precious. He bowed and gave it to me. "Yours, I think, Miss Louisa."

Again I was looking up at those brilliant blue eyes.

I forced myself to look down, glancing at his fashionable coat and white stock and then the length of his legs in the immaculate and skin-tight pantaloons which emphasised his manhood.

I was afraid that my blushing face would give me away. "Thank you, Sir. You seem good at catching things." My voice shook a little.

"My pleasure." He bowed. "I could hear your voice, true and strong even when the choir was singing. I enjoy singing myself."

Bet nudged me as our parents came up. "How did he find the church?" she whispered.

"You both look like angels ready for Heaven," he said. "But I hope not just yet."

"Sir – we meet again," the Captain said to Mr. Edsir. "And on such a special day for your lovely daughters. How fares your elder daughter and the baby?"

Mr. Edsir looked up at him, a surprised expression on his face. "They do well, Sir, and I thank you again for bringing the surgeon."

Mama Edsir bobbed a curtsey. "My warmest thanks for your help, Sir."

Susan, her mother, and Miss Wildbore came out of their special door leading to their private pew. Lady Tyrconnell was leaning on Miss Wildbore's arm, coughing as usual. The Vicar and the Bishop, robes blowing in the wind, fluttered over to them like plump and brightly-plumed birds.

"Excuse me, Sir," Mr Edsir said to the Captain, before he hurried his wife away to speak to the Tyrconnells.

Bet went to speak to Will and his wife so we were alone in the windswept graveyard.

He took my hand. "Please – Miss Edsir – Louisa – we must

101

meet and talk. I want to know you much better. Seeing you here in church, looking so beautiful, has only increased my feelings towards you."

I couldn't move my hand, while a strange thrill went through my entire body.

"Sir – I don't know. It might not be possible," I whispered.

"Please. I do so need to talk with you. I want to know all about you." His voice was urgent, pleading.

I saw Bet and the others moving towards us, carrying shawls against the cool wind. Dick was with them, his face set and angry.

My heart was racing – I wanted to see him so much. It was time for the new Louisa to be bold. "I could bring my sister to the Mill – by the river Mole. After six of the clock tomorrow."

"I shall be there." He raised his hat, bowed, and walked away swiftly but he was waylaid by Susan, who smiled up at his height as she talked to him.

I was trembling and not just from the cold wind. I had just escaped from Archie Malham and now I was making an assignation with an unknown soldier. Supposing Bet refused to come with me? I would certainly lose my good name if anybody saw me alone with the Captain in such a secluded place.

"Are you feeling faint, Louisa?" Susan was there, smiling. "Did the good Captain upset you? Isn't it strange that he came all the way from his Army camp to a Confirmation in our little village? I told him that you were in demand and that Lord Archibald Malham was paying court to you."

I turned on her furiously. "Why did you have to say that? I have refused Lord Malham's attentions."

"I didn't want him to think you were just a humble farmer's daughter, whose head would be turned by a handsome Scots-man."

"I find him very charming."

She laughed. "My mama saw you talking to him and she

reminded me of your circumstances. She still won't tell me the truth of your birth but others have remarked that our gestures and smiles are alike. As we wondered – you're probably a poor and distant relation and in that case, not allowed to throw your reputation away for an unknown Army officer." Then she smiled. "Even if he is quite delicious! And you are right, he is certainly better than my Earl or Lord Malham." Then she looked serious, for once and looked away at her mother, whose was leaning on her husband's arm, coughing. "I fear my mama may be seriously ill, for all she still preens herself to see her lover. We need to go home." And she hurried off.

There was no time to talk to Bet as the entire Edsir family except for Martha and the new baby crowded into the farm to drink beer, cider and that expensive luxury, tea, sent by the Tyrconnells and served in Mary Edsir's prized bone china cups.

As we handed round slices of cake and gingerbread, I was sadly aware of Dick glowering at me but I could do nothing about his jealousy.

"So what was the Captain saying to you?" Bet asked as we refilled the platters.

I took a deep breath. "He wants me to meet him. I said I would come with you to the river, if you agree."

Bet was about to cut into a second plum-cake. Now she waved the big knife in the air. "So what if I refuse? Dick saw you with the Captain and he is upset already. Supposing I tell him what you plan?" She plunged the knife viciously into the cake.

"Bet – why have you turned against me?" I couldn't believe the change in my sister.

Bet put down her knife and held my shoulders, as if she wanted to shake me. "I think the Captain may be up to no good. If he wanted to pay court to you, he would come to the house. No, he thinks you're just a farm-girl and easy to seduce. If you aren't careful, he'll leave you with a baby on the way."

I wriggled out of her grasp and tried to speak lightly. "Hardly possible with you as a chaperone! Besides, I do have a will of my own."

"There are men who will take you against your will," Bet said. "Remember poor Annie Rust and that stranger from London? Her ma threw her out and she died in the workhouse, having her baby."

"I remember. But that's enough, Bet. A girl of your age should not know such stories."

Bet tossed her head so hard her muslin cap fell over one ear. "You forget I'm now fourteen, not a child. Anyway, I will think on it. If you care for our family at all you won't meet him."

One of the many Edsir grand-children had come in the kitchen and a small hand reached for a large slice of cake. The little boy ran off giggling.

The tension eased as Bet ran after him, calling his name.

I felt shaken in my resolve. Supposing I waited at the Mill and he didn't arrive after hearing about Lord Malham? Would I dare go there if Bet refused? And supposing Bet was right? The Captain looked to be only a few years older than me and had no need to marry yet. If he did – surely he would chose someone out of his own circle?

Then I thought sadly that he might get killed in battle. Did I want my heart broken by a soldier who was never at home and might be in danger?

CHAPTER 15

"You are not listening to me, Louisa," said Miss Wildbore. "I asked you to recite the sonnet by William Shakespeare. You were supposed to have learned it by heart."

I wanted to tell the governess that my heart was already engaged. I had been staring out of the window at the distant lake, now lit by a shaft of sunlight piercing the clouds. The night before I had hardly slept, even with Tobias snoring beside me for comfort.

"I'm sorry, Miss Wildbore. I forgot," I said.

Susan smiled knowingly. "Her thoughts are elsewhere, I believe."

"I know the sonnet," Bet recited it slowly and carefully.

It was all about love...

"Love is not love which alters when it alteration finds
Or bends with the remover to remove
O, no! it is an ever-fixed mark
That looks on tempests and is never shaken..."

These lines stayed in my mind. If the Captain was falling in love with me he would not want to alter my background and nothing would deter him. I told myself not to be such a romantic. He was attracted to me, that was all. And how did I feel? Rather more than mere attraction, certainly, and I knew I would be greatly disappointed if Bet was right, and his plan was seduction.

When we were leaving Claremont, Susan came after us. "I

forgot. There's a letter for you, brought by hand. It's sealed with the Bilsborough crest."

I wanted to tear it up but it might not be wise so I slipped it into my pocket.

"That's Lord Malham's family, isn't it?" Bet asked as we went to find Dick and the dog-cart. "He hasn't given up trying, has he? I wonder why he didn't send the letter to the farm."

Dick sat quiet and hunched on the way back. He hadn't mentioned the Captain's unexpected arrival at the church but at last he spoke, his voice so quiet that Billy's hooves clattering along almost drowned it.

"That Captain Macdonald who came unbidden to your Confirmation. Is he trying to win your affections, Lou?"

I felt indignant. I was sixteen, not a child for Dick to order about. He was jealous. But again I knew I was cutting myself adrift from him, from my brother and best friend.

"I have no idea." My voice was cold. "And in any case, he will be going away to Ireland soon."

Dick merely grunted and flapped the reins on Billy's haunches, causing him to trot so fast that we were soon rattling and bumping over each rut in the road.

As soon as we returned, I escaped to my room and opened the note from Archie Malham. It was just that, a curt note, not a letter.

> *Miss La Coast – if you will not see me I shall tell your father you forced me to come with you to the Conservatory, knowing we would be alone – where you flirted with me, putting your arms round me even though I protested. If I put about this story you will lose your reputation and never find a husband. I have gathered you are a bastard child, secretly fostered but I was willing to ignore this and give you my ancient and respected name*

and a life of ease.
                    Archibald Malham

Bet came in. "What's the matter, Lou?"

I tried to hide my angry tears. "It's this note from Lord Malham." I could hardly bear to say his name.

"What did he say?"

I gave her the note.

"You are well rid of that gentleman!" Bet tore it up before I could protest. "If he can call himself a gentleman! Don't answer it. He won't dare dirty your name and nobody would believe him anyway."

"Like mother like daughter," I said bitterly. "That's what they will think. My mother may have been seduced, but perhaps she was at fault. Perhaps she was no better than a…" Then I couldn't go on.

Bet hugged me. "Don't think about it, Lou. I wish I was a man and I'd challenge that Lord Malham to a duel! I'd thrust my sword right into his black heart!"

I tried to smile at her but I was wondering if Captain Macdonald might hear of this false rumour?

"Lou dear, you've hardly eaten anything," Mama said after supper. "And you're so pale. I hope you aren't sickening for a fever like Bet's." She fussed with her hair and her lacy cap, as she did when she was worried.

It was true, I felt sick. "It's nothing but a passing headache. I need some air, Mama. I will take Tobias for a walk, if I may. Do you need flour or oatmeal from the Mill?" My heart was beating so fast I wondered if it showed.

Mama went to look in the store-cupboard. "I suppose an extra bag of oatmeal would be useful," she said. "Take Bet with you. It will be sunset soon and all kinds of beggars and ruffians have been through the village lately, to say nothing of the soldiers. And wear your shawls against the evening chill."

Tobias, as usual, led the way to his favourite walk, his tail wagging its white plume.

"So I had to come with you anyway," Bet grumbled as we crunched through the fallen leaves. Yesterday's wind had dropped and the trees were still, as if they were already going to sleep for the winter. Squirrels chattered and streaked up the trunks like small puffs of red smoke.

Only one couple passed us, leading a donkey with laden panniers. "If you're wanting flour, you need to hurry," the woman said. "Miller's off to the ale-house at Stoke very soon."

"That's good. He's a right gossip," Bet said.

Perhaps she was on my side, after all.

Tobias stopped and sniffed the air, looking back. I was so nervous that I turned round but saw nobody.

When we came to the river, the evening sun shone low through the trees. The dark water was patterned by fallen leaves, yellow as gold coins. We followed the riverside path to where the mill-race gleamed white in the gloaming.

We were near the mill when I said, "Wait." I drew Bet into the trees as I saw the Miller come from his doorway and move along the opposite tow-path towards Stoke.

"Well, where's your handsome Captain?" asked Bet.

"He may not come. Perhaps he has had second thoughts." I felt a stab of sadness but also a curious relief at the thought of returning to our safe home, instead of stepping out into the unknown.

Tobias, nosing along the bank ahead, wagged his tail and barked as a red-coated soldier came riding round the curve of the river.

My legs felt weak and I clutched at Bet. "What shall I say to him?"

She pushed me away. "Lou – you arranged this meeting. You tell folk you are sixteen and a woman now. This is your chance to show it."

And she began to walk back. "Don't go!" I pleaded.

"I'll wait on the path for you – unless you scream, then I'll come!" Bet called back.

He was waving at me!

Tobias barked even more loudly and sprang from the bushes, making the horse shy and I was shocked to see the Captain fall off. The horse came trotting on towards me but I managed to catch the loose reins and lead him back a few paces to where the Captain was already struggling up, his coat splodged with mud from the tow-path.

"I'm sorry my dog scared your horse. Are you hurt?" I don't know why but I put out my hand and he grasped it and sprang to his feet.

He still held my hand firmly, saying, "Only my pride and my clothes!" He laughed. "We're doomed to meet, Miss Louisa, falling off horses. Thank you for catching Brutus."

The horse moved forward at that moment, almost pushing me right up to the Captain, who still held my free hand.

We stood close and I did not want to move away. I looked up at his face and saw the tenderness and something else in his expression, something which made his eyes soften and glow.

"Please, Louisa," he said in a husky voice and bent down to my small height, kissing me lightly. His lips were soft but firm and I found I was kissing him back, giddy with the scent of him and with this totally new sensation.

He released me and sighed. "Oh, Louisa! So you do care a little, my love? How long can we stay? And where is your sister?"

"Just a little way off." I wanted him to kiss me again and again but I told myself this must be the wanton streak in me.

"Will she miss you for a short while?"

"No, Sir," I said, out of habit. I couldn't think of Bet or any-thing but him at this moment.

"Call me Godfrey, please, my love."

He tied the horse to a sapling growing by the path. "Shall we take a little walk?" he asked, taking my hand.

The river glowed red and gold, reflecting the setting sun and an owl called mournfully. Soon it would be getting dark and Bet would come to fetch me. I stumbled on a clod of earth.

"Hold my arm, dear Louisa, if you please," he said.

There was something in his voice that made me obey but with pleasure. He was so tall that I had to reach up to him.

"Tell me about yourself, Louisa," he said. "You said the Edsirs were only your foster-parents? And yet they have given you a different name."

I felt the miniature in my pocket. If he knew the story, he might not want to see me again. But I wanted him to know the truth, lies or half-truths would come between us. "I don't know who my parents are," I said. "I was left as a baby with the Edsirs, who have brought me up like one of their own. I think I may be a distant connection to the Tyrconnells, as they have often called with gifts for me. Now I share their governess with my sister and Lady Susan but nobody will tell me the truth."

"I find that very sad." Godfrey said.

"But I've been happy…" I began

"Except you wonder why you were abandoned."

"I do, from time to time – more often now I'm older. Did you have a happy home?"

"Yes. I was born in the fair city of Edinburgh and I had nine brothers and sisters."

"And your parents?" Suddenly I wanted to know all about him.

"Sadly, they are both dead. But we were a happy family."

"I'm sorry. But at least you knew them and they loved you."

Suddenly he stopped and put both hands on my shoulders.

"We can console one another. Louisa – I have fallen in love with you from the moment I saw you. Could you care for me?"

I was filled with warmth and joy. "Yes," I said, without hesitation.

He kissed me again, this time with passion, which I returned, gathered up in his arms. I wanted to stay there for ever but I forced myself to move away, thinking of Bet's words about seduction. I knew then, that I was as tempted as he was.

"I'm sorry – I'd like so much to stay close like this… but I cannot…" my words were confused, my voice wobbling.

"I know what you may be thinking," he said gently. "But I'm a man of honour and I want to marry you."

"Marry me? I have no dowry." My heart was beating so fast I could hardly breathe. "And you hardly know me!"

He laughed. "I have only my Captain's pay at the moment but I don't care a fig for your lack of a dowry! And I feel I have always known you. I want to spend the rest of my life loving you and learning more about you each day."

Then he kissed me again, lightly, many times. "I adore your nose, your chin, your forehead," he murmured – and your lovely mouth."

Tobias was running up to us, barking and we moved apart.

"I think he's heard someone," I said.

He turned. "There's nobody in sight but we don't need to hide, my dear love," Godfrey said, still holding me tight. "I plan to ask your foster-father if I may marry you. Once we are engaged we can see each other every day. I want to talk to you, make you laugh, make you happy."

I felt dizzy with joy, then I thought of Farley Edsir and how he wanted me to marry Lord Malham, even if I didn't love him. "He seems to want me to marry a rich man with a title. But I will stand up to him – after all, I'm seventeen in January."

My cap had fallen off and my carefully pinned up hair had fallen down. He stroked it. "I'm not rich but I can look after you. I wish we had more time to persuade your foster-father and also for a leisurely courtship but I have to join my Regiment in Ireland in the New Year and I want to take you with me."

"Ireland. I have never been further than Guildford!" Happiness sang in my heart. "We hardly know each other, though, do we? Just these few meetings."

"I know you're sensitive, kind and loving – I saw that when you were so concerned about your foster-sister. I think you like children? I'd like a big family eventually and they would all be good-looking and sing beautifully like you. I imagine listening to my family making music on winter evenings…"

I could picture the scene, myself at the harpsichord. "I've always wanted children. But I didn't want to marry until I was older."

"And now?"

"I feel differently." My voice was muffled by his kiss as he drew me up again, close to him, and I was filled with that new and strange longing.

Then I drew back a little. "First, I have something to confess to you." I took a deep breath. "I met Lord Malham at Claremont. He's tried to court me against my will, even asking my foster-father if we could become engaged. Now he's written a distressing letter saying if I don't agree – he will put about some story that I almost forced him to a secluded place and made play for him."

Godfrey looked horrified. "My poor Louisa! How could he do such a thing – try to ruin you! Where does this gentleman live – if you can call him a gentleman and not just a rotten seducer? I need to teach him a lesson." He sounded really angry.

I clutched at his arm and felt the hard muscle under his coat. "No! Please don't try to see him. It will make matters worse. My foster-father likes him because he's the son of the Earl of Bilsborough and will inherit big estates."

"That matters not a jot to me! I belong to the ancient Clan Macdonald and in the past, we have fought our enemies to the death. I can scare him off quite easily."

Papa would lock me up for good if there was a fight! "No – please leave it alone. I hope it's an empty threat."

"He can't do anything if he knows we are engaged to marry. Dearest Louisa – say I may ask Mr.Edsir's permission for us to wed. I want to start our life together very soon."

He held me close again and I felt myself melting, almost as if we were already one body and spirit. "Yes," I whispered.

"Oh, Louisa!" And he kissed me again.

Then I heard someone calling me. A familiar voice. An angry voice.

"Lou! Come home at once."

It was Dick.

CHAPTER 16

The light was fading fast now but it was good enough to see Dick's angry face as he ran up to us, Tobias at his heels.

"You're to come home at once, Lou," he shouted. "And you, Sir, ought to be ashamed, compromising my sister by seeing her alone, and in the evening." Fists clenched, he scowled at Godfrey

I couldn't move.

"Your sister has accepted my marriage proposal," Godfrey said quietly. "I shall speak to your father. I hope we can be friends in the future, Dick." He smiled.

Dick still glared at him. "Lou's far too young for marriage, Sir." The last word sounded mocking. "And we know nothing of your family. It could be an empty promise."

Godfrey took my hand. "I'm a man of my word from an honourable Scottish family."

"So you say." Dick's voice was rough. "You're a man, Captain, for all that and my sister's been alone with you in this place."

"Dick – please, no more anger," I pleaded, holding back tears because I knew his anger wasn't just for my reputation but because he loved me. "And where's Bet?"

"When you were so long, she was fearful and ran back to find me and she did right, as you were bent on ruining your-self with this gentleman." Again there was a subtle sneer in the word.

Any joy I'd felt earlier with Godfrey was destroyed – was I a wanton girl, perhaps like my mother? "I have to go back," I

114

whispered to Godfrey.

"Don't be fearful. You have done nothing wrong." He looked over my head at Dick, who was blocking the narrow footpath. "I intend to speak to Mr. Edsir this very evening." Without warning, he lifted me onto the horse's back and mounted behind me, holding me with his free arm. "The path is rough and the light fading. You might trip, my love."

I hadn't the strength to protest.

Dick had to move as the horse walked forward. "I'll tell my father," he shouted. He'll send you off!" Then he was gone, running ahead of them into the darkling wood.

"Remember, whatever happens, I love you. Will you love me always, Louisa?"

For a moment, all my doubts fled. I would remember this moment all my life.

"I will. Always."

My words were carried away by a gathering wind, shaking leaves like wedding flowers over us.

I leaned back against him, safely wrapped in the warmth of his coat, feeling his strength flow into me.

As we approached the farm, my mood changed and I began to worry. Godfrey was strong and persuasive but my foster-father was already angry that I had refused rich Lord Malham.

It went badly from the start. Mr. Edsir was summoned from his study, where he was dozing over the accounts he kept for the Duke. He looked both angry and surprised to see me with the Captain, who wasted no time in getting to the point, after bowing and smiling politely.

"I have come to ask, Sir, if you will permit me to marry Miss Louisa. I know she's very young but she has given me the honour of agreeing to spend her life with me."

We were in the hall and I was only too conscious of Mama, Tom, Bet and Dick, all shadowy figures in the candlelight.

"Louisa, please retire to your room," Mr. Edsir's thundered. "Sir – will you come to my study."

Godfrey took my hand. "Do as your father bids." He lowered his voice. "I will not give up, whatever happens."

Bet lit a candle and followed me upstairs.

"Why did you fetch Dick?" I asked her.

"Because you were so long." Bet chewed a strand of escaped hair. "I was scared – we don't know the gentleman. He might have taken you away."

"I wish he had."

"You would leave us – leave me? And for a stranger?" Bet was almost shouting.

Tobias, sensing a quarrel, jumped up, growling, and Bet loosened her hold.

"Godfrey doesn't feel like a stranger. And it would be very hard to say goodbye to you all." My voice broke. "I love this family, even grumpy Papa."

"I can tell you, your Captain hasn't a chance with Pa. He's had a letter from Lord Malham. I recognised the seal when I collected it with other mail, left at the Brown Bear Inn."

"And no doubt he will be telling lies about me." I was so angry I paced the room.

We could hear Papa Edsir's loud voice now, coming through a hole in the floor-boards. "No!" he was shouting. Then his voice faded. Was he ushering Godfrey to the front door?

Mama burst into the room carrying an oil lamp which she put on the dresser. She hugged me close to her plump body which smelled of lavender, of cooking and sweat.

"You have sorely riled Mr. Edsir, Lou. First, you refuse rich Lord Malham and now you want to marry a complete stranger."

I tried to talk calmly. "We've met several times, Mama. And remember how the Captain helped us fetch the doctor for Martha, as well as stopping my horse bolting. He is a kind, good man and we love each other."

Mrs. Edsir hugged me so close I felt the bones of her stays. "Lou – I didn't really approve of Lord Malham because I think you're too young to wed."

At that moment I heard the front door close and a horse clopping away.

He had gone without a word.

I burst into tears as Dick knocked on the door. "Pa wants to see you in his study," he said. "He has given that gentleman short shrift," he added, with some pleasure.

I went downstairs, shaking but still determined.

"Come to my study and sit down, Louisa." Mr. Edsir thundered.

The smoky room felt full of spent anger as I sat on a low stool.

Papa's voice was loud and angry. "I have sent your suitor packing. He's neither money nor title and only speaks of an uncle with a castle on a far-away Scottish island, no doubt filled with wild heathens. I totally forbid any idea of a betrothal."

I looked up at him, defiantly. "Then I will never marry."

"You will do as you are told. I've told him you must marry a man of rank and fortune."

"Why, why, why?" I shouted.

"You need not know. Just that I have to obey someone of great rank. I have told Captain Macdonald never to approach you again."

I stood up, filled with desperate anger and sadness. The old Louisa would have obeyed her Papa but I screamed, "I will see him!"

His face was dark red as he shouted back, "You will obey me, Louisa La Coast, and go to a boarding-school until you see reason. I've had a letter from Lord Malham. He says you deliberately led him into a conservatory and made improper advances. But he's prepared to overlook your behaviour if you will become engaged to him. You need not marry until you

117

are seventeen."

"His story is a lie! I would rather throw myself into the river rather than marry that man!"

And I stormed out of the room, tears pouring down my face.

CHAPTER 18

I lay in a kind of black stupor, Tobias by my side, hardly noticing when Mama came in with a bowl of pottage and dry bread.

"'Tis all Mr. Edsir will allow, my love." She apologised. "And I'm to lock the door." She was crying as she hugged me. "His heart is hardened. He's riding to the school tomorrow to arrange that you go there at once."

"I won't go!" I turned my head into my pillow.

"You have to, my dear. But you will be sent back here for Christmas. And you will have other girls' company at the school and continue with your education. At least he is not going to force you at the moment to become engaged to Lord Malham. You'll soon forget the young Captain. After all, you hardly knew him."

Supposing he really did love me and came back to the farm to find me gone? It seemed such a slender hope that he'd seek me out after leaving so abruptly. I had to tell him the name of the school, all the same.

I tried to speak calmly. "Where am I going?"

Mary Edsir patted my shoulder. "Don't worry, my dear. It's a very respectable establishment run by two sisters. Mr. Edsir knows a merchant whose daughter is there. I think the name is Winter Hall. It's very near Guildford, about an hour's coach ride away from here."

"Can Bet come too?"

"No – we can't afford to send her as well."

"Will she visit me with you?"

Mama wiped her own tears away with her kerchief. "Mr. Edsir says you are not to receive visitors as a punishment. But I shall persuade him, Lou. He may think he rules our roost but I often find a way. I go deaf when he talks – I don't make his favourite dishes and – I might even retire to another room at night."

"I hate him!" I shouted.

Then I saw the hurt on her face. "Please don't say that, my love. He is a good honest man and thinks he has to protect you and see you make a good marriage. And – as for myself – I love you as a daughter and I don't want to lose you to any man, so young."

"I love you too," I said. "I remember when I used to call you Mama-Nursey, long ago." I hugged her, then there was a shout from below.

"He wants me. He's upset too, you know." Mama went out and I heard her locking the door.

I ate a spoonful of the pottage but the bread stuck in my throat and Tobias finished it up. Surely someone would come? I hammered at the door and called out, "Please, don't make me a prisoner!"

There were voices below.

Then the key turned in the lock and Bet came in, with a jug of warm water.

"I persuaded Pa that you would need to wash. Oh Lou, I am so sorry I brought this on you! As I said, I was afeared in the dusk and you with the Captain." She put down the jug and I held her as she sobbed, "I don't want you to go away. Pa won't let me go too."

I tried to comfort her. "I know. I wish you could be with me. But it's November now and I shall be back for Christmas, Mama says. Bet – if you go to Claremont tomorrow, can you tell Susan where I shall be? It's just possible that Godfrey – the Captain, may ask her. Unless our angry father has put him off altogether." My voice broke then.

"Perhaps Pa will change his mind once you are seventeen," Bet said.

"Perhaps." But I didn't think it at all likely. "And if Archibald Malham comes – don't tell him where I am. And does Dick know I'm being sent away?"

"Yes. He tried to argue against it but Pa flew into one of his rages. Poor little Tom was sent to bed, crying."

Again I tried to speak calmly. "You'd better go, dearest Bet. Come in the morning. After all, Tobias needs his food and to go outside."

When Bet had gone, I felt very alone and exhausted by the emotion that was tearing me apart. "I need to make a plan, Tobias," I said, talking to him as I often had in the past.

He licked my face clean of tears, then sat, watching me.

It was cold that night and I hugged him to me, trying to get warm. In the past, Mama would have brought me a warm brick, wrapped in a piece of blanket.

I wondered if I could run away. But where to? I could hardly wander Bagshot Heath looking for Godfrey's regiment, and that would probably bring disgrace to him. If only I could talk to him.

There was still money left in my purse, even after paying the doctor. I decided to take it with me to this dreadful school, in case I had to bribe someone to get a letter to Godfrey. Then I realised I didn't know the address of his Regiment, except it was at Bagshot Heath.

While it was still early and almost dark, I heard a clattering outside in the stable-yard. Farley Edsir must be on his way to the school.

I must have dozed then, despite my misery, but I was woken by the key turning and Bet came in. "He's gone to Winter Hall – what a gloomy name! He won't know if you come down for a while, so long as you get back in time. Ma went to bed late and she's still sleeping. The key was in his study."

We went quietly downstairs.

Annie was in the kitchen, making porridge. "Miss Louisa – there was a mighty lot of talking last night and I heard you're going off to live in a school. You'll be sorely missed. I'll do up some honey cakes and cheese for you. Them places isn't so good on food, I've heard."

"Thank you." I realised how much I would miss old Annie and the warm kitchen. I kissed the old woman, surprising her, so she nearly knocked the pot over.

I was trying to eat my porridge when Dick came in. "So, Lou, you're being sent away?" He put his warm hand on my shoulder.

"Against my will."

"And I didn't agree to it either," he said. "But Pa had the bit between his teeth."

I couldn't eat any more. "I'll miss you a great deal."

"You will? More than you will miss that Captain Macdonald?" His eyes staring at me, seemed hard.

I couldn't answer.

"That's not fair, Dick," Bet said. "Lou's fallen in love with the Captain, like it or not. You're a dear brother to her."

"Like a brother but not a brother," he muttered. "I thought of Lou as more than my sister. I'd hoped…" He slumped down on a stool and didn't finish.

I hated seeing him like this. "You and Bet are my best friends and I can't bear to leave you," I said, trying hard not to cry.

Dick sighed. "That gentleman did you no good, Lou. At least you will have time to think on it."

Then we heard the clatter of hooves. "That's Pa coming back," Bet said in alarm.

I wondered for a moment if I ought to face him but I'd get Bet into trouble for taking the key from his desk so I went upstairs, telling her to put the key back. I didn't really care that Farley Edsir would find my door unlocked – if he came upstairs.

I looked out of my window at the familiar stable-yard and the fields beyond. William and his dog were herding the cows to the milking parlour. Would I see him again?

Tom was in the yard, leading Papa's horse to the stable. Even from here, I could see the cob was sweating from fast riding.

I leaned out of the window, waving at Tom and softly calling his name.

He grinned and waved back. "You be punished enough, Lou?" he asked.

"I have to go away," I called back. "Please could you send my love to Will and the others. And look after Bertha for me."

"Don't go, our Lou!" His face crumpled, as if he might cry.

I heard Papa Edsir's voice thundering below. Then Tobias scratched at the door. I opened it and he came in, proudly carrying a thick envelope in his mouth.

I told him how clever he'd been and gave him a piece of oatcake and he let the package fall in my hand. Nobody had fetched any letters from the Inn – left by the Mail Coach – so this must have been delivered by hand.

It was sealed. For a moment, I thought it was Lord Malham's and then I saw the seal bore a different crest. Perhaps the distant shouts I'd heard were from Mr. Edsir, who had seen Godfrey ride by.

Feet were creaking up the stairs so I ripped the letter open quickly.

"*My dearest love,*" it began and then the door was opening. I thrust the slightly soggy letter into my bodice.

Mama bustled in, carrying another bowl of porridge. I forced a smile and almost told her I had already eaten but then I remembered Bet would be in trouble for letting me out of the room.

"Mr. Edsir must have forgotten to lock the door," she said, handing me the steaming bowl. "Try to eat this, Lou dear. Mr. Edsir is back, saying the Misses Winchester are pleased for you to join their school. He speaks well of the house and says there are ten girls boarding, so you won't be short of friends."

"When?" The smell of the porridge made me feel sick.

"He stopped by at Claremont this morning and they are sending a coach at noon with Lady Susan and the Countess to travel with you. Such an honour – you will arrive in state, Lou dear!" She smiled. "It was not thought fitting for old Billy to take you in our little trap – besides, the pony is so slow now. I will help you pack your clothes."

I was to leave at noon. I had to read the letter and somehow let Godfrey know where I was going.

I clutched my stomach. "Mama – I have a pain. My monthly courses... I need the privy." I didn't like deceiving her but I had to read the letter.

She looked concerned. "You poor dear – and on such a day! I will brew you ginger tea and find your clouts. But promise you will not run away."

There was nowhere to go.

CHAPTER 19

It was cold and smelly in the privy and I heard mice scuttling away when I sat on the wooden seat. It was not a good place to read a letter from my love.

He might be telling me he was not my love and never could be, after Mr. Edsir's angry words. Again, I wondered what had been said, to make Godfrey ride away without a word to me and I had a real pain now, but in my heart.

There was a small lump enclosed, wrapped in cloth.

I unwrapped a signet-ring, bearing his crest.

His writing was firm and legible.

> *My dearest love,*
> *I have no ring for you but my own. Please keep it to plight our troth.*
>
> *I must see you but Mr. Edsir would turn me away, so we shall have to contrive a secret meeting. I still have hopes you will agree to marry me now. This means we shall have to elope to Scotland where you will be allowed to marry under age, unless your foster-father relents. I am not good enough for you, he says. I asked why and he revealed to me the secret of your birth but I would rather tell you face to face as I feel it will be a shock for you. I feel angry about the whole affair. I want you by my side now – I cannot wait that long time until you are of age.*
>
> *This is written in haste as I have to see my*

*Colonel. I shall come back to the village later
today. Perhaps you can contrive to send a letter
to the Brown Bear Inn if you cannot escape to
meet me by the Mill again. I shall go to both
places before noon.*

With all my heart and soul, Godfrey.

My thoughts whirled but my pain vanished as I knew he still
loved me. My foster-father had told Godfrey the truth about
my parents but wouldn't tell me – why?

How could I get a letter to the Bear? If only I could have
seen him just once before I left. Now he wanted me to elope
to far-away Scotland and then go to Ireland with him, leaving
the home I had known for sixteen years. I knew that once I'd
left with Godfrey, Farley Edsir would never let me return.
Forgiveness was not in his nature and in fact, he might send
Dick to go after us and bring me back.

How could I bear not to see my dear family again? For
them, it would be as if I had died. He would probably forbid
them to mention my name again.

"Lou! Are you in much pain? I have the clouts for you to
wear."

I opened the privy door. Bet was outside.

I decided to tell her the truth. "Godfrey has written to me. He
wants me to elope with him to wed in Scotland."

Her face went red, then pale. "How could he ask you to do
that? It's a plan to seduce you. Don't listen to him. Besides,
what about us? It's bad enough, Pa sending you to that school
but at least we shall see you at Christmas."

I tried to put my arm round her but she moved away. "He's
sincere, I'm sure. He really does want me to be his wife but I
do feel pulled apart – I hate the thought of leaving you all and
the hurt you would feel if I ran away with him. But I love him
so much and I know I shall never marry unless I can be his
bride."

"Rubbish!" Bet shouted. "Of course you will marry one day – unless you want to help me run a school? Wouldn't that be wonderful, Lou?" She looked happy at the thought, dear Bet, still a see-saw of emotions. "Come inside, now."

I turned to see Farley Edsir glowering at me from the doorstep. "Come here at once," he shouted, so loudly and angrily that he set Tobias off in a frenzy of barking.

I hated him at that moment.

His face was a turkey-cock red as he almost pushed me indoors. "You will obey me, Miss, and stay in your room until the coach arrives. His Royal Highness the Duke of Gloucester" – he rolled off the title with enjoyment – "has summoned me to Hampton Court. So I shall bid you good-bye."

I stood very straight and stared at his angry dark eyes. "You're so cold and unforgiving, Sir. And yet you pose as my father. Before you send me away, you could at least tell me the truth about my parents."

"I am bound not to do that. And I don't like your manner, Miss La Coast. You are going away for your own good, to forget about that presumptuous Captain Macdonald." He put his hand on my shoulder and his voice was a shade warmer. "You will be missed. But if you behave, you will return for Christmas."

Then he turned away, walking down the cobbled path to the stable yard.

Bet had been hovering in the background. "Lou – he's been horrible to you but I think he really will miss you," she said.

"Bet – aren't you going to your lessons at Claremont?" I asked.

"Dick has gone already, riding Billy." Bet said. "I don't want to go to Claremont alone now you are leaving."

"Bet! Please – you're clever and want to be a schoolteacher. Don't let me spoil your plans."

"They may not want me now you are gone." She drooped

127

sadly.

"Of course they will. Susan is lonely and you make her laugh. Now – I have to write a letter. Can you persuade Ma to let me say goodbye to Will and Daisy – and to Bertha."

"Pa said you were to stay in your room."

"He'll never know. I will write the letter." I ran upstairs to my room. Mama was just fastening the straps round the straw travelling basket.

"Are you feeling better, Louisa?" she asked. "You must tell them at the school that you are indisposed." Her hair had come down again and I felt a pang, as I saw it was going grey. She was getting old – if I went away with Godfrey, I would never see her again.

I felt a pang of guilt as I said, "The pain's gone but I need to rest for a while."

She went out, giving me a sorrowful look. I went to my desk.

I was so cold that my writing wavered as I wrote to Godfrey:

> *My love,*
> *I shall send this to the Inn for I am kept in my room until the Tyrconnells' coach comes to take me to a boarding school at noon. The school is called Winter Hall and is somewhere between Esher and Guildford. I know no more.*
>
> *Your letter brought tears to my eyes. I am going to wear the ring on a silken thread round my neck to show we are betrothed.*
>
> *Do you know Shakespeare's sonnet with the lines…*
> *(love) "is an ever-fixed mark*
> *that looks on tempests and is never shaken."*
> *This is how I feel.*
>
> *I wish I could see you but it seems impossible – and so does your plan for us to elope. I want to*

128

be your wife but I do not wish to hurt this family,
who have cared for me.
   Would you wait for me?
   My heart is yours.
          Louisa.

I tried the door. It was not locked so I crept downstairs with the letter. Bet and Mama appeared to be arguing loudly in the kitchen. I went into Mr. Edsir's study, where a small fire burned in the grate. Taking his sealing-wax from his desk, I lit a taper, and melted the wax, so I could seal the letter with the signet ring.

I wrote his name on the folded letter, care of the Brown Bear.

Bet came in, looking rumpled and tearful. "You shouldn't be here, Lou – bad enough me going to his desk. I've persuaded Ma that Tom and me'll take you to the dairy to say goodbye to Will."

We found Tom in the stable yard, mucking out a stall.

I hugged his thin little body to me. "I shall think of you, little brother."

"It's not fair, making you go away," he said, sniffing.

I showed him the letter. "Would you take this letter to the Brown Bear Inn for me, please, dear Tom? It has to be a secret."

Tom pulled at his wild hair – a habit he had when he was worried.

"A secret from Pa?" he asked. "Because he is sending you off? I hate him for it and I'll take the letter and never breathe a word."

I gave him a two pence for the Landlord of the Inn and one for himself. When he ran out of the yard, I wondered if I would ever see him again.

I found Will in the dairy with Daisy, finishing the milking. Will, always a man of few words, just said, "Tis a darned shame, our Lou."

Daisy smelled of milk and cows when we kissed. "He didn't ought to have sent you off," she said. "It fair makes me angry to think on it."

Then Bet and I went to see Bertha. It seemed a long time since that carefree day when I brought the piglet back from the Fair.

The sow came running to my call, grunting with pleasure when I scratched her back. I smiled and turned to Bet. "Promise you won't let Papa kill her at Christmas."

"I'll try," she said but she looked doubtful and I felt a small sorrow adding to my burden.

Then Mama was calling me back to change for the journey.

"You will wait in the parlour for the coach, dear," she said.

At last Tom came back, panting, leaving a trail of mud and straw in the parlour. "I ran all the way, Lou. Your Captain was there, waiting. He gave me a silver sixpence too. Now I am rich! And he said" – He scratched his head. "Something – I forget."

I couldn't bear it. "Please, try to remember."

"He said something funny like he would never give up. And there was a bit about his heart but I had to run back before you went."

When the coach arrived, Tobias, anxious at the tears and farewell hugs, sat on my foot to stop me going. "I refuse to go without him," I said firmly.

"He's your dog," and Tom heaved the spaniel up and into the coach after me.

Lady Tyrconnell gave a faint shriek as the muddy spaniel spattered her dress.

When I looked out of the window, I saw the three Edsirs standing there, crying and waving before the rain and mist hid them.

I had never slept away from the farm before and sadness gripped me so hard that for a moment I couldn't speak. For once, Susan didn't chatter but put her arm round me. I apologised to Lady Tyrconnell for my muddy dog. The Countess merely nodded between coughing and taking sips from a silver flask. Then the feathers on her hat drooped forward as she slept.

"What happened?" Susan asked softly. "Don't worry – she's taken laudanum. She won't wake for a while yet."

My voice was hoarse with tears as I explained why I was going away and also about Archie's threats. "Supposing he hears of Godfrey's proposal and writes to him? Supposing Godfrey then has a change of heart?"

"Oh, my poor Lou!" Susan said, so softly that her voice was almost drowned by the horses' hooves and the clatter of harness. "Your foster-father just said you were going to a very good school. Miss Wildbore heard and was most upset and I'll miss you so much. I can understand why you love Captain Macdonald – he's so handsome even if he has no money. Archie Malham's behaviour is vile and you are well rid of him. Your Godfrey wants you to elope. It's so romantic!"

"Yes, but I'm to be imprisoned in that school and he won't be able to see me. He may just give me up and depart with his Regiment." I wondered why Susan wasn't paying attention but looking out of the coach window as we approached the Brown Bear Inn.

"Look!" Susan was pointing at a horse and rider coming out of the inn's courtyard.

My heart raced. "It's Godfrey!"

He urged the horse on and soon was riding alongside the coach. He smiled and raised his hat. I pulled down the window and leaned out.

His horse tried to shy to one side but Godfrey tugged the rein and put something in my hand. "I love you!" he called loudly.

Lady Tyrconnell woke with a start. "Close the window at once! The cold air will make me ill," she ordered. Then she sighed and closed her eyes.

I was clutching the folded note as the coachman whipped the horses on, trying to overtake the mail coach. I looked back at Godfrey before the thickening mist hid him from sight.

"Oh, how exciting! I thought he would hold up the coach like a highwayman and take you away!" Susan whispered as I unfolded the note. "What does he say?"

I showed her.

> *"I will never give you up. Loving you always,*
> *Godfrey."*

CHAPTER 20

"We do not usually take in pets." The owner of Winter Hall, Miss Mercy Winchester, nudged Tobias away with her toe as he sat beside her, mouth half-open to catch the crumbs of a dainty cake she was eating.

Her eyes looked like small black currents in a bun and she was so fat she seemed as if puffed up by a bellows. I thought she might explode if you stuck a hairpin into her.

"I must keep Tobias!" I cried.

Miss Mercy looked down at the dog, frowning and shaking her head. Tobias, always pleased with any attention, put a large paw on her skirt and wagged his tail.

"Miss Louisa has to keep her dog," Susan said in a haughty voice. My father said she was to have every amenity. Is that not so, Mama?"

Lady Tyrconnell opened her eyes, nodded and then coughed into a lace handkerchief. "Every amenity," she whispered.

"The dog must be with her at all times," Susan went on relentlessly.

Miss Hope Winchester, the younger sister, was stick-thin and quiet but she put her hand out to Tobias and stroked his head.

I tried to drink tea from the delicate china cup but I was too upset to relax. This parlour was carpeted and warmed by a fire but the school hall was ice-cold and the prospect of the tall grey-stoned house, surrounded by a high spiked wall had depressed me immediately. The gates were shut when we arrived but a huge iron bell-pull brought a gaunt old man who opened them, shutting them immediately behind the coach.

"We hope to visit Miss Là Coast very soon," Susan said.

Miss Winchester shook her head and forced a smile. "Lady Susan – I am afraid we do not allow visits for at least three weeks, so our pupils may settle down."

Susan gave me an almost imperceptible wink and put on her most frosty voice. "My father, the Earl, may very well request a visit before three weeks."

I knew that Lord Tyrconnell was away very often and he certainly would not want to come to Winter Hall.

Miss Winchester's fat face was creased with smiles. "In that case of course His Lordship…His Grace…" She stuttered, confused. "He will be most welcome."

Lady Tyrconnell began to cough again and Susan said they would have to leave. She gave me a scented hug. "Write to me," she said in a low voice.

When they had gone, the Winchesters took me to a long dormitory, warmed only by a very small fire at one end. There was a row of iron-framed beds, each with only a thin quilt on it and a small dresser beside. In the middle of the room was a marble-topped table, set with jugs and basins.

"You may put one book or object on your dresser," Miss Winchester said.

"Where are the girls?" I asked. "They're very quiet."

"We do not raise our voices here and there is no talking at meal-times," Miss Winchester said. They are at present in the Refectory. You may join them."

"I'll show you the way, dear," her sister said, taking my cold hand in her own bony one.

"Wait, sister. Miss Winchester waved a fat arm. "First, Louisa must hear our rules." She counted them out on her fingers. "One – you will wear the uniform you will find on your bed. Two – all romantic novels are banished. Three – your letters home come to me first. After two weeks, you may be allowed out on a supervised walk. Four – and this is most important – no gentlemen are allowed to visit the pupils. Five

134

– unpunctuality for lessons or meals will be punished. Six – all food must be finished. Seven – no pupil is allowed to wear jewellery." She looked at the twisted skein of silk which looped round my neck. The signet ring hanging from it was hidden in my bodice.

"Come, sister. The girl must be famished." Before her sister could comment, Miss Hope Winchester marched me away, saying, "My sister is rather too strict. You will be happy to know that we have singing classes, practise deportment, learn poetry and of course study the Bible. There is even a harpsichord."

I wasn't greatly cheered, especially when I saw the girls silently eating in the dining hall. They all turned to look at me and I wanted to run away.

A pale-faced servant girl gave me bread and thin soup, followed by a small piece of strong-smelling fish and one potato. A skinny girl dressed in a sludge-brown dress with a demure white collar was standing, reading aloud from the Bible.

"You have to eat it all," whispered the girl next to me. She had chapped red hands and limp dark hair.

Tobias had slunk after me and I waited until Miss Winchester had turned away, slipping the fish to him under the table.

I cried into the hard pillow that night and was only comforted by Tobias, snoring beneath the bed. Home seemed far away and dear Godfrey even more remote.

How could I escape?

CHAPTER 21

It was the worst time of my life. The weather had turned even colder, with icy winds creeping ghostly fingers through the ill-fitting windows and doors. A tiny fire was lit in the so-called 'recreation room' but it did little to warm it. Everyone huddled in shawls and some wore mittens as well. I was used to a cold bedroom at the farm, where the fire was only lit when you were ill, but in cold weather Mrs. Edsir always wrapped towels round hot bricks so at least we were warm in bed.

Most of the other girls seemed subdued and some giggled when they heard my stupid surname, so I asked to be called Louisa Edsir.

Worst of all, I had no word from Godfrey – or perhaps he had written and Miss Winchester had opened the letters.

"Has anybody asked to see me, Miss Winchester?" I asked.

"There was a letter but I sent it back as Mr. Edsir instructed."

I was angry. "You had no right to do such a thing!"

Miss Winchester's face crumpled with rage. "How dare you speak to me like that, Miss La Coast! You are under age and in our charge. No recreation time for you, Miss. Go to the schoolroom and write "*I will obey the rules of Winter Hall School,*" fifty times."

One night, Kate, the girl in the next bed, whispered, "Three weeks and it will be Christmas and we go home. I have hated the school from the first and I've told my family I cannot come back here because I am always ill."

I liked Kate straight away. Like some of the other girls, she was the daughter of a merchant who wanted her to acquire the airs and graces of the Gentry. She had a cough as bad as Lady Tyrconnell's but tried her best to make me laugh and took me down the back stairs, early one morning, to find meat for Tobias in the dark kitchen.

Mrs. Jackson, the harassed cook, obviously tried to mother Kate. "You need feeding up, Miss," she said. "That Miss Winchester's as mean as a miser. I don't know how she expects me to feed you all. Well, don't tell on me." She gave Kate a slice of seed cake. "Meant only for Her Highness and her sister but what she don't know, don't harm her. And you have that there dog to feed, Miss Louisa."

Tobias, who had been sitting quietly, put a pleading paw on the cook's lap.

I put money in Mrs. Jackson's hand, saying, "I can pay for him."

"No need for that." All the same, the cook put the money in her apron pocket and gave Tobias a lump of fatty meat and a bone to take away.

One of the servants was a thin girl who came to stroke Tobias and I asked her name. She bobbed a curtsey. "Maria, Miss," she said.

I smiled at her. "Maria's my second name."

"Is it? Fancy that, Miss!" She grinned, showing great gaps in her teeth.

"She's a good girl," Mrs. Jackson said, "but far too young for such a lot of work. Came from the Orphanage, she did, with another skivvy but that one caught a fever and died."

"That were a scandal, hushed up" said the bent old man who had opened the gate. He was carrying a heavy basket of frosted cabbages and carrots.

"How's your bad back, Silas?" Kate asked.

He groaned. "Never worse. I don't mind helping in the kitchen and suchlike but I have to take coals upstairs, dig these veg and then walk a good mile to the Angel at Guildford to fetch the post left by the mail coach and I only got that no-good boy to help me. When I asked Her for more money she says would I prefer the Workhouse at my age?" He wiped his nose with blue-tinged fingers. "Frost's that terrible outside."

I suddenly had an idea. "Could you take a letter to the Angel Inn in Guildford where the Mail Coach calls, Silas? It's very important."

"She'd find out," Mrs Jackson said. "Eyes in the back of her head. Fancy calling her Mercy. Well, she don't show any mercy to nobody."

"No, she don't," Silas agreed.

I offered him more money. "Just once," I pleaded.

Like the cook, he took it quickly. "Tomorrow. Give it to Maria for me."

A voice boomed out from the doorway. "And why are you young ladies in the kitchen?"

I thought Miss Mercy Winchester would really explode this time.

"No breakfast for you both and please to copy a Psalm and learn it before lessons begin," she ordered.

Tobias growled softly at her.

"And take that dog out to the shed."

"He can't stay there. It's too cold," I said but Miss Winchester went conveniently deaf.

Kate decided to stay inside as she was coughing.

Miss Winchester unlocked the front door. "Out," she said. "The animal will be perfectly all right in the shed."

I had no intention of leaving Tobias outside but I was glad to get out of the house. Each day I'd been allowed to let my dog out into the garden for a short time but Miss Winchester had held my arm in iron fingers, forbidding me to follow, as if I might scale the high wall and run away.

The other girls had been taken out in a shivering crocodile while I was kept inside but a storm had prevented any of them going to church last Sunday.

A thin winter sun sparkled on a magical world. Tobias nosed

the white-frosted grass, rushed into the frost-rimmed bushes, then emerged to gallop round the garden, his tail wagging with joy.

I hoped that a letter sent by coach from Guildford might reach the Brown Bear. There was just a chance Godfrey might call there. Suppose he thought my silence meant I'd changed my mind?

I longed with all my heart to see him but this long wait had filled me with doubts. What had Mr. Edsir told him about my parents? Was there some secret disgrace in the family? I wanted to know the truth but at the same time, I feared it.

Calling Tobias inside, I went up to the schoolroom where Kate was sitting at her desk.

"I need to write letters," I told her.

"She reads them all. Be careful what you say," Kate opened her Bible and began to copy a Psalm.

I wrote quickly to Godfrey, addressing it to the Brown Bear Inn at Esher and praying he would call there.

> *My dear heart,*
> *The dreadful Miss Winchester who runs this*
> *school tells me she sent a letter addressed to me,*
> *back to Mr. Edsir. I hope this letter will reach*
> *you, sent from the Angel Inn at Guildford. I long*
> *to see you but you won't be allowed to visit me.*
> *We have been kept indoors owing to inclement*
> *weather but next Sunday we walk to St.Martin's*
> *Church in nearby Chalworth. I believe I shall be*
> *allowed out at last.*
> *Please come.*
> > *My dearest love,*
> > *Louisa.*

I wasn't going to copy the psalm because I'd done nothing wrong. Instead, I wrote to Susan.

139

Dear Susan,

Please come and see me soon! This is a cold and unloving school where the food is as poor as the lessons.

If you should see the Captain, please ask if he received the letter I have sent to the Brown Bear.

Tell Miss Wildbore the harpsichord here is out of tune and I am only allowed to play hymns. Our time is spent mending the school's coarse linen and copying out Psalms – and learning how to address the Nobility, like you, Lady Susan! Miss Mercy Winchester talks a great deal about God but I think she only worships the angry God of the Old Testament.

Louisa

Please share this letter with Bet, if she still attends lessons and tell her I love and miss her. I am writing to her but Mr. Edsir may prevent her reading it.

I hope Lady Tyrconnell's health improves.

The girls were singing a hymn at the end of the service following breakfast. So I just had time to write a short note to Bet:

My dearest sister,

I hope you will receive this letter but fear Mr. Edsir will intervene. I miss you all so much. Whatever happens, please remember I love you and have been happy at the farm.

My fondest love to you, Mama and the family.

Louisa.

I put the folded letters in my pocket just in time as Miss Winchester marched in and demanded to see our work. I told

her I refused the task and she ranted at me but I closed my
ears.

CHAPTER 22

Silas took the letters with a great deal of grumbling. I found the hard bed worse than usual as I tried to sleep. In four days' time we would all walk to the village church. Would Godfrey come? And if he did, what would I say to him? I replayed vivid memories of our last meeting again and again, remembering his deep, loving voice, his firm mouth on mine, the stirrings of desire in my body, spiced with the excitement of the unknown.

If I saw him and he still wanted me to elope, could I ask him to wait until January? I longed to see the farm one last time, especially at Christmas and to say goodbye to all the dear familiar people and places which had filled my whole life until now.

I felt so divided. If I went with him, I would have to leave the south of England. I'd said I wanted to go further than this small part of Surrey but now the prospect of travelling so far away made me feel almost dizzy.

What had that gypsy said at the Fair? "You will need strength and courage to go with your love." Had I that courage? All round me, the girls were sleeping, some snoring and I felt so alone. As if he guessed, Tobias jumped on my bed and licked my face.

On Saturday afternoon, Maria came to the students' draughty day room to say Miss Winchester wanted me in the parlour.

The teacher's fat face was creased with smiles. "Lady Susan Carpenter is here to see you, Miss La Coast – with her maid."

In a moment, Bet was hugging me so tightly that she nearly knocked me over.

"Elizabeth is not my maid," Susan said with a reproving look at Miss Winchester. "She's Louisa's foster-sister." She smiled and kissed me.

Miss Winchester frowned but summoned Maria, ordered tea and then paid Susan fulsome compliments.

I whispered to Bet, "Did you get my letter?"

Bet nodded. "Your – friend – called but Ma turned him away. She was afeared Pa might lay into him. I slipped out and told him about the letter awaiting him at the Brown Bear."

"That was kind."

She looked sad. "I still don't approve of him wanting to take you away, Lou. Best you forget him."

"Is everyone well?"

"Yes. Tom says to tell you Pa said he would kill Bertha for Christmas."

"Oh no! How could he do that? – it must be to punish me."

Bet touched my hand. "It's all right. Tom enticed her with carrots and led her far off to the woods where there are acorns aplenty for her to eat and where we've seen wild pigs. He made a kind of shelter of boughs and will take her food until she's settled. He told Pa and Will she'd escaped through a hole in the fence."

Silly tears came into my eyes hearing that Tom risked a beating. "Please thank him. I hope she'll be all right. The wild pigs might kill her."

"Or she might mate with one!" Bet said hopefully.

She was quiet while they drank tea and she refused a slice of plum cake. Bet usually had such a good appetite but now she seemed troubled.

Miss Winchester chattered on: "The weather has been inclement recently but Miss La Coast will be joining the pupils for church next Sunday, weather permitting. It is but a short walk from our school."

143

The light was fading and Susan said the horses found the roads very icy – they had better go home before dark. "I have a box for you, waiting downstairs," she said. "And here is a warm cape."

I smiled gratefully as I took it and felt the soft fur lining.

"Christmas presents, Lady Carpenter?" Miss Winchester bared her teeth in a smile.

"Not exactly." Susan frowned and I hoped she wouldn't refer to my complaints about the school or I might be kept indoors on Sunday, as a punishment.

Susan was looking at the red chilblains on my fingers. "There's a fur muff in the box, Lou. You need one for the cold. And I've asked my Mama if we can bring the coach to collect you on Christmas Eve."

I thanked her but wondered if I would ever go home.

Miss Winchester had seen Susan looking at my hands and twittered on about having fires in all our rooms. She never added that they were small and only lit in the evening.

When they were going out, Bet whispered to me, "You will come back for Christmas? It's only five days away. We're decorating the house with pine boughs and there's a wonderful smell of spices from the cakes and pies being baked. I had a bad dream that you won't come. That I might never see you again. Please don't go away with the Captain."

"Bet – I can't promise anything." I was trying not to cry.

Then both Winchesters were there, bidding Susan goodbye as if she were Royalty.

The coach was at the door, driven by Carter, two footmen riding pillion.

Bet looked back once, as she and Susan went. I tried to smile at her.

The Winchesters went into to their warm parlour and Maria came up to me. "Don't you want your box, Miss Louisa?"

"Yes – of course." But it seemed unimportant. No doubt it contained cakes, sweetmeats, and the like but the muff would be useful.

"Let's open it in the kitchen." I didn't care that I might be in trouble, going below stairs again.

I wanted to go home.

Then I thought of losing Godfrey's love and the sadness was like a cold stone deep inside.

CHAPTER 23

I felt sick with anxiety and couldn't eat any breakfast that Sunday morning.

It was bitterly cold and I was glad of the fur muff and the lined cape. Kate coughed beside me in the crocodile. I'd confided in her that Godfrey might possibly come to the church so she had insisted on being with me. "I'll distract the Winchesters so you can speak to him," she declared.

The servants following, we picked our way with care along the icy road leading to the church, our breath clouding the frosty air.

There was a sudden cry. I looked round and saw Miss Winchester had slipped and fallen. Her sister pulled her up but she was limping badly. "Silas shall have to help me take her back," Miss Hope said as the girls gathered round and she put the two eldest in charge.

"This will help you, Lou – getting rid of the Winchesters," Kate said as we stumbled and slid on our way.

Various carriages, gigs and dog-carts waited outside, their drivers covering the horses with blankets. A ragged village boy held a bay horse's head and my heart beat fast. But this horse was smaller than Brutus.

A chestnut mare was tied to a post, reminding me of Folly and that reckless ride when Godfrey saw me fall.

Would he come?

As the school-girls filed into the church, the choir sang an Advent hymn with music composed by Bach, reminding me of playing Bach at Claremont, before my whole life changed.

When we filed out at the end of the service, I looked for Godfrey, hoping he might have come in late. Then I was so shocked and surprised that I stood still.

Dick was standing at the back.

I pressed myself against the side of a pew as the girls pushed past but I had to get out quickly. There was a press of people talking outside the door and I hoped to escape but heard Dick calling my name.

Then he was there, his hand on my arm and drawing me into the porch. The girls walked past us, giggling and staring.

"Bet told me you would be here." His voice was rough and urgent. "As I am not allowed to visit the school, I rode here. Lady Susan loaned me Folly."

"It's good to see you." My voice shook. I was conscious that the older girls were waving and calling me from the lych gate and the others had already left. The Vicar, wrapped in a cloak, was frowning at us.

Dick pulled me behind a buttress. "Bet says the Captain will try to meet you. Please, dear Lou, don't run off with him. We want you with us for Christmas. Remember, we all love you." And his expression softened.

I hated his coming here and making me think of home. "I love Godfrey," I said simply.

Then, there he was, as if I'd conjured him up, Godfrey Macdonald striding up the path towards us. Dick saw him too and before I could say anything, he was hurrying down the path and confronting him.

What were they saying? Somehow, on strangely weak legs, I stumbled away into the churchyard and sank down on a tomb sheltered by a yew tree.

Would they fight? Surely a stable-hand would never attack one of the Gentry?

I had not been able to eat breakfast and now as I looked up into the dark yew, my eyes blurred and I fell into blackness.

Then strong arms were pulling me up. "I couldn't find you,"

147

Godfrey said. "You fainted. Can you walk now, my love?"

I was pressed to his great-coat, my bonnet falling off as he kissed me and my body flooded with new warmth. Then I realised where I was and heard the carriages move off, harnesses jingling. A distant voice was calling me.

"Did Dick strike you? Was there a fight?" I asked urgently.

Godfrey looked down into my face with a tender expression. "No. But I think your foster brother wanted to hit me, he spoke so angrily. Could he be jealous?" He stopped.

I didn't know how to answer but I hated to think of Dick's hurt and disappointment. We had been so close and now I might never see him again.

"Louisa, my love." Godfrey hesitated.

The snowflakes whirling down seemed to cut us off from the noise of departing carriages.

I had dropped the muff but Godfrey took my kid gloves off my cold fingers and held both my hands in his warm ones.

"I have to tell you the truth," he went on "I told Dick that I was determined to marry you and nothing would stop me. He said his father disapproved of me so I told him the secret of your birth. I think he was ashamed of the lies you have been told. So he mounted his horse and rode away. 'Tell Louisa I shall always remember her,' were his last words to me."

I wanted to cry. Then I heard someone again calling me. "I have to go. Please tell me quickly about my parents. I have to know."

He held me close. "I hate to upset you but you have a right to know. This is what Mr. Edsir told me: King George's brother, the Duke of Gloucester, is your father, and your mother is a certain Lady Almeria Carpenter, sister of the Earl of Tyrconnell. Susan Carpenter is your cousin."

The words shocked me. "I don't understand. Is my mother alive still?"

"Yes."

The word seemed sharp and bitter like a blow.

148

He went on, "I will put it boldly. Your mother, Lady Almeria, is the Duke's mistress. Mr. Edsir felt I was not good enough for you and made the point that I am merely a Captain in the Army and as a younger son, may not inherit title or lands. He was looking for someone of a higher rank."

I was so shocked I could not speak. "The Duke of Gloucester…" I remembered that ugly Duke who had glared at me outside Hampton Court. He was my father.

"Perhaps he forced my mother to abandon me."

"Perhaps."

"But she's alive and has never once come to see me. And my mother, this Lady Almeria, left me with strangers." I remembered the gypsy's words and murmured, "My mother was like the cuckoo who will never know her fledgling." My voice tailed off as I remembered kissing the miniature portrait, feeling my mother must have loved me, even for a day.

"I know. It's very hard." He held me very close "I'm here now for you. I've only one question. Do you love me enough to run away with me to marry and live with me until death do us part?"

He kissed me again, lingeringly, his lips cold from the snowflakes and his love began to heal the huge shock I felt, learning that my beautiful mother just did not care to see me, nor my father to acknowledge me.

Then I knew Godfrey not only my first love but also my last love, and nothing else mattered.

"Yes. I love you more than enough," I said softly.

He spoke urgently. "It must be soon. I have to rejoin my Regiment in Ireland very soon. I'm lodging tonight at the Angel Inn, in Guildford – only a mile away from here."

I tried to think quickly because I could see a figure coming towards me through the swirling snowflakes. "The school is like a prison and the gates are kept locked unless someone is expected. I shall have to find the key."

"I'll hire an extra horse and we'll escape by night to Guildford, then wait for the mail coach which goes to London, then another to Carlisle."

I remembered Tobias. "I have to bring my dog. He'll be treated cruelly if I leave him behind."

"We'll take him too. I shall leave Brutus at the Angel Inn and hire a gig. The whole journey should take about five days. When shall it be? Soon, my darling, please, while I still have leave. I could take you now, on my horse."

I was alarmed at his wild idea. "In daylight! We would be seen and I'd be brought back. You might be disgraced and even jailed for taking me away."

He smiled. "Soldiers have to take risks. I so desperately want you to be with me – soon. It will have to be in darkness, I suppose. Tonight?"

I saw Kate hurrying towards us, half-hidden by the falling snow. "I have to go back now," I told him. "It may be hard to get out of the school but I'll try tonight. There's a big bush growing near the wall outside. Wait by there near midnight. If I can't escape then, I'll try tomorrow night."

He gave a gasp of pure joy. "That's wonderful and so brave of you! But if I don't come, it will be that nobody will loan me a horse and trap because of the bad weather. I know this is so difficult for you, my darling." He held me so close that his signet ring, hanging round my neck, pressed into my flesh.

"Yes." I admitted. "I'll be escaping into a new life, a strange and different life."

"But with me."

"Yes. With my dear love." I sealed my words with a kiss.

I looked up to see Kate was staring at us, her mouth half-open with surprise.

Godfrey raised his snow-covered hat to her and smiled. "You're Louisa's friend?"

"Yes, Sir. I'm Kate." I could see her looking at him with approval. "I have been sent to fetch her back. The others are on their way because of the snow."

"My horse would take you both, Miss Kate," he offered. "Nobody will notice in this weather."

She smiled at him. "Thank you, Sir, but Louisa will be in enough trouble as it is."

Everyone had gone when they came out of the churchyard gate. "Please wait a moment." Godfrey went to fetch Brutus.

Godfrey took the rug off his horse and, laughing, put it over our heads. "Tell them you found it lying in the snow. Go carefully." He touched my cheek in farewell, then mounted.

I hated seeing him disappear into the white snow-curtain.

"Oh, he is so handsome!" Kate said as we slithered along, snowflakes blurring our sight, the horse-smelling rug over our heads. "And such a commanding way with him. One look from those blue eyes and you want to obey."

"He's strong in all ways but he has a kind and loving heart." I hesitated, then said, "I have to tell you – we plan to elope, tonight if possible."

"How exciting! But how…"

"I'm making a plan. You mustn't tell anyone."

"Of course not. And if I can help? I can give you money…"

I thanked her, then became silent as thoughts whirled round my mind.

Now I knew that the Edsirs had lied to me about my parents, I felt a little better about leaving the farm. I tried to forgive Farley Edsir, who perhaps had to obey his master, the Duke of Gloucester.

But it was hard to take in all Godfrey had told me and I tried not to feel bitter about my parents totally ignoring me. I'd heard that the Duke was married, so he very likely wouldn't have wanted his wife to be hurt by finding his love-child, but he could have come to see me secretly, as could my mother.

It was strange to think the King of England was my uncle but I was pleased that the lively Susan was my cousin. I felt so sad and angry about my mother's neglect but at least she wrote that note, asking to keep me safe. Perhaps that ugly Duke had forced her to give me away.

I resolved that if our plans went well and we married – I would try to forget the parents who had forgotten me.

But I would keep the miniature.

Half way back, we were met on the road by old Silas, leading the Winchesters' small dog-cart, pulled by an old and sagging pony. Cursing under his breath, he bundled us into the cart.

"I been sent to fetch you," he said. "Madam is in a right rage, Miss Louisa. Where did you get that horse-blanket?"

I didn't answer.

As the pony slithered back through the snowstorm, I pushed resentful thoughts about my parents away and thought only of Godfrey, my true love, his deep reassuring voice, his compelling eyes and sensitive mouth. If we managed to elope, we would marry and have children who would know and feel secure in the love of their parents.

I shivered and not just from the cold. Would I have the courage to run away with him? Supposing I was caught? Godfrey would be disgraced and I would probably be sent away to a distant and even worse school.

I told myself that the new Louisa would overcome fear.

CHAPTER 24

"You have brought disgrace on our school." Miss Winchester's small black eyes shone with anger. Her ankle was bandaged and she had her foot on a stool. Her sister stood beside her, looking anxious. "You were seen with two men and then you ran off."

"One was my brother," I said defiantly.

"And the other? Your father told us that you were sent to us to keep you from a totally unsuitable soldier."

"He wants to marry me." I was swaying as I stood, faint with hunger and emotion. "And the Captain is an honourable man."

Miss Winchester rapped on her desk with her cane, which she sometimes used on our hands in the classroom. "I will hear no more. You will be locked in a room and kept there until you apologise and promise you will do no such thing again."

"We want the best for you, dear," her sister said feebly. "You will have your books."

Tobias chose that moment to scratch at the door. "And my dog," I said.

"No dog," snapped Miss Winchester.

I remembered her weakness for titles. "Lady Susan Carpenter will be upset if I tell her how you are treating me."

"Very well. You may have your dog. Now, go. My sister will take you down."

"Down where?" I realised I ought to have apologised because it would be much more difficult to escape now.

"The room is in the basement," Miss Hope Winchester looked upset. "But I shall see you have food and Maria will come to remove the chamber pot and bring you water for washing."

I knew Maria would help me but I had to write a farewell letter to Bet. "I shall need ink, paper and quills, please Miss Hope." I tried to smile.

She patted my shoulder. "Yes, dear. I will take them with us. But do realise my sister will read any letters. Besides, you won't be here for long. The Christmas holiday is only a few days away, when the school closes. Of course, if my sister tells your parents of your meeting with the gentleman – they might request that you stay here for the holiday."

"That's impossible!" I found my fists were clenched. But I remembered I would be gone with my dear love by then, God willing.

I went to the empty dormitory to pack some clothes and special books into my wicker basket. I wore my cloak and hoped the Winchesters wouldn't see me, or they might be suspicious that I was trying to run off. Then I needed to get a message to Kate, who had been sent to join the others at evening prayers. I intended to ask Kate to help me escape as it wouldn't be fair to burden the little maid, Maria – she might well be sent back to the orphanage in disgrace. Kate was leaving the school so she wouldn't care if she got into trouble.

The basement room was down a damp corridor from the kitchen, next to a store room where I knew Silas slept on a mat.

I had thought to escape through a window, but that was barred. The stone floor was bare, save for a rush mat. At least Miss Hope had put ink paper and quills on the wooden table. The rest of the room was furnished with a battered chair and a rusty iron bedstead.

It was ice-cold. "The room hasn't been used lately," Miss Hope said apologetically.

"Shall I light the fire, Miss?" Maria had come with us, bringing a bowl of water and a bone for Tobias, from the cook.

"Yes indeed," said Miss Hope Winchester. "The room is cold – and please bring Miss Louisa bread and soup for her supper. But be sure and lock the door when you go." She called Silas. "Bring coals, please and watch that this young lady doesn't wander off."

When Miss Hope had gone, Silas leered at me and laughed, sounding like a rusty saw.

"We'll see yon pretty young bird doesn't fly the coop, won't we Maria?"

"I don't like such talk, Silas," Maria's voice was sharp. "T'aint respectful to Miss Louisa."

Silas brought the coals and it was then that I saw the bunch of keys dangling from his belt.

When he had gone, I spoke to Maria, who was trying to coax the fire into life.

"Would you please ask Miss Katherine to come and see me after prayers with my own clothes and tell Silas he has to open this door for her?"

"I'll straightway do as you ask, Miss," Maria said. "I hates to see you shut in a room like this. Mrs. Jackson thinks it's a crying shame. We'd both leave the school if we could find new positions – but that witch would never give us references."

When Maria had gone, I wanted to cry but forced myself to stay calm.

The fire had barely warmed the room so I wrapped myself in my cloak. Tobias sat on my feet again, nervous that I would leave him in this dismal place.

The early darkness of December filled the room and I could hardly see by the one candle, throwing strange shadows round the room.

I put the candlestick on the table next to the quills, ink and paper. I had to write and say goodbye to Bet.

155

I dipped the quill in the ink and began writing, cramped with cold.

> *Dearest Bet,*
> *Please tear up this letter after you have read it.*
> *They have imprisoned me in a cold room but I plan to escape very soon. Godfrey and I shall be wed. Please, after I have gone, give my love to all the family, even Mr. Edsir.*
> *I will remember them and especially you, dear Bet, when I begin my new life as Godfrey's wife.*
> *With all my fond love, and best wishes for your future,*
>
> > *Lou.*

Now all I had to do – all! – was to get out of this room – and somehow get the key to the gate from Silas.

It was all so difficult. For just a moment, I longed to be back at the farm and enclosed by my safe country life.

Then I thought of Godfrey and felt the dizzy longing and the warmth of my love for him flooding through my whole being, like a river bearing my fears away.

I heard voices and the key turning in the lock. Kate burst into the room and rushed to hug me.

"Oh my poor Louisa! Imprisoned in this dreadful room. I'm so glad I'm leaving this school. My parents have sent word to say they are coming tomorrow to take me home."

"Kate, my darling friend." I hugged her. "You kindly said you'd help me escape. And now you see I am locked in. Would you come down here when everyone's asleep, and unlock this door?"

Her thin face lit up. Yes – of course I will! It's so exciting!"

"Would you tell the Winchesters in the morning that you unlocked the door? Otherwise, they'll blame Maria and she'll suffer."

"I'll be glad to shock old Sourface! She can't do anything to me now I'm leaving. Rely on me, dear Lou. I shall miss you a great deal." She kissed me, then looked at the table. "You've been writing a letter. I'll take it to the nearest Post Inn."

I smiled at her. "I hoped you would. And thank you for making me laugh, even in this dreadful school."

"I have to go and pack now. I think Maria locked me in!"

Kate called and the little maidservant unlocked the door, locking it carefully again as soon as Kate had gone.

Maria came to take Tobias into the garden. When they came back, sprinkled with snow, I whispered, "Does Silas keep the keys in his room at night?"

"Yes. And he sleeps sound if he's had Mrs. Jackson's elder wine. She'll bring you your soup for she's sorry for you, then ask her to open her wine for Silas." She gave a sideways look at me. "You be going to your love? I saw the fine gentleman waiting outside the church."

"I hope so. Oh, I wish I could take you with me and fatten you up, Maria."

"Don't you worry about me, Miss. I be friends with the butcher's boy. He says he'll marry me one day."

When I gave her the few groats I had left, Maria thanked her as if she'd won a fortune. "God go with you, Miss," she said.

Mrs. Jackson came in carrying a laden tray. "She – that Miss Mercy, ordered just thin soup and bread." She snorted. "That woman! I've added butter and cheese and a piece of cake meant for her. She stuffs herself while everyone else has short commons."

I decided to trust Mrs. Jackson. "I have to escape," I said. "Can you get Silas to drink plenty of wine tonight? I need to get his keys. Miss Kate will open this door for me. She is leaving the school and says she will take the blame."

Mrs Jackson enveloped me in an onion-smelling hug. "I will fill that sour old man to the brim with wine, Miss! And I wish you God-speed and to be happy with your love."

When she had gone, I shivered with nerves.

"Do you think my plan will work, Tobias?" I asked him.

He looked up at me with his big brown eyes and slowly swished his tail.

"I hope you're right," I whispered as the fire went out and the only warmth in the room was the dog, lying on my lap as I waited for midnight.

CHAPTER 25

Despite Maria's efforts with the fire, it gradually died to embers. I sat on the hard chair, determined not to go to sleep. I'd changed out of the school's coarse brown linen dress into my own clothes, wrapping myself again in my cloak. I would need to take the oil lamp with me – I had discarded the wicker case as being too difficult to carry but I'd take the fur muff against the icy cold. I wrapped the miniature in a kerchief and put it in my pocket.

Soon, all sounds of feet above disappeared as the girls went to their dormitory, the young ones first and then the older girls, like Kate. I guessed that Miss Winchester would go to bed early, after her fall, and Miss Hope always did what her sister wanted. It was still a guess, though and I would be taking a risk.

I heard Silas' loud voice in the kitchen, mingled with scraps of out of tune singing and then his clumsy feet, staggering down the corridor, muttering a rude ditty. Very soon his loud snores filled the basement.

Mrs. Jackson's wine had done its duty.

The house was silent. Would Kate escape from the dormitory undetected?

I heard the faint sounds of the Grandfather clock in the hall above, and counted eleven but still Kate didn't come.

Then there were light footsteps and the key turned in the door.

"Thank you," I whispered as Kate looked in, wearing her nightgown.

"God speed," she whispered, blowing me a kiss before she crept back upstairs.

I put on my leather boots, gathered everything ready and tied Tobias to the table, telling him to wait.

I opened the door as quietly as I could and tip-toed down the cold stone corridor, carrying the lamp. It was easy to follow the snores and also the smell. Silas lay on a pallet in a corner of the store room. He oozed an overpowering stink of wine and his own unwashed body.

I held the lamp high but I couldn't see his belt and the keys. Did he go to bed wearing them? I shuddered at the thought of pulling the filthy blanket off him and probably waking him. His dirty feet stuck out of the bottom of the bed.

Then I saw the glitter of keys, thrown down with the belt on the other side of the straw mattress. As I leaned over Silas, his stinking breath made me retch.

He groaned and turned over, muttering something. Was he waking up?

I grasped both belt and keys and crept away on shaky legs.

Back in my room, I undid the leather thong that bound keys to the belt. Four keys, two large, two small. Which of the large ones opened the gate? I tied them to my waist-sash for safety, in case I had to run.

Tobias whined softly so I untied him. My heart beating fast, I slipped out of my room and into the kitchen where Mrs. Jackson and Maria slept behind a flimsy screen next to the fire. Would I wake them, opening the door? Then they would find it hard to pretend they hadn't seen me escape.

The kitchen door was bolted fast but dear Mrs. Jackson must have greased the rusty bolt and it opened easily.

Tobias pulled me out into the ice-cold air and my feet slipped from under me. I found myself in a heaped up pile of snow, dug from the path. No light – I must have dropped the oil-lamp and it had gone out.

Snow filled my mouth and panic flooded my body. I'd kept

hold of the leash and I told Tobias to go forward. He pulled me out and made for the big black gate.

A thin crescent moon and a scattering of stars gave me a little light so I could just make out the key-hole. I tried the biggest key but the lock wouldn't turn.

Tobias was snuffling and whining at the gate. Would someone hear? I looked back and thought I saw a candle lit high up, where the Winchesters slept.

My frozen fingers shook as I tried the second key. It fitted but it took all my strength to turn it and I had to throw myself against the huge gate to push it open against the fallen snow.

Then we were outside.

I just managed to push the gate shut behind me in case the Winchesters looked out, and saw it open. Then I threw the bunch of keys into the snow as a last gesture of defiance.

"We're free, Tobias!" I whispered.

I shuffled through the snow to the bush, which had turned into a big white snow-hump. When would he come? I was already shivering with cold and fear.

Tobias was nosing under the snowy bush and I found a kind of hollow underneath the lower branches, dry and filled with dead leaves. I pulled the dog after me and curled up, as best I could, melting snow dripping down my neck from the bush. I curled round Tobias for warmth, my hands in the fur muff.

Time went by, so slowly. Would we freeze to death? Why didn't he come? For a moment I longed to be safe and warm at the farm. Then I told myself to be brave, just as Godfrey must have been when he faced the enemy in battle.

The cold seeped through me and I felt so tired. All I wanted was to sleep but I knew I had to keep awake and move a little or I would die.

An age passed, and I half-dreamed of home, of the river and the Mill on a warm summer's day. Then Tobias licked my face so I woke from the deadly slumber.

There was a muffled sound of wheels and horse's hooves

outside.

"Are you there, my love?" Godfrey's voice.

Something had happened to my legs – I just couldn't move.

Tobias heard Godfrey's voice and jerked at the leash, pulling me out to tumble into the snow, unable to walk.

"You are half-dead with cold." He was picking me up and taking me in his arms to the horse and gig. "Oh my poor dear love," he whispered.

"Tobias!" I called weakly.

"He's following," Godfrey said.

There were two oil-lamps at the front of the gig and I hoped nobody would see the lights.

Was that a voice calling out?

He covered me with his great-coat, warm from his body and leaped onto the driver's seat, urging the horse on, slipping and sliding on the snowy road.

My new life had begun.

The drive was short but perilous, as the gig was light and once almost overturned on the frozen snow, the jolt extinguishing one of the lamps.

He held the reins with one hand and took off his glove. His fingers crept into the warmth of my muff and laced with mine and I felt loved and safe.

Then for a moment, I realised I would never see Martha's baby grow up – never find out if Bet became a teacher – nor whether Susan married the man she secretly loved. Tears came into my eyes when I thought of Mrs. Edsir's kind face which I had known all my life. I might write to the family but I felt certain they would not reply.

His hand came out of my muff and touched my cold cheek. "My dearest – you are crying. Are you regretting coming away with me?" His voice was soft and almost uncertain and I thought of him as a strong and determined person.

"No regrets." My voice was husky. "I want to be with you, always. But it's sad to leave old friends."

"I know. I am tearing you away from all you have ever known. When we have a home, babies, friends, the memory of your old life will fade."

He kissed my cold lips. "We're nearly at the Angel at Guildford. I shall ask for mulled wine to warm you while we wait for the Mail Coach to take us to London and thence by other Mail Coaches to Scotland."

The houses and cottages were a huddle of darkness but there were oil-lamps and candles burning in the lower windows of the Inn as we drove through the archway into the cobbled courtyard.

A boy took the horse and the dog leaped out as Godfrey helped me down. I was so stiff with cold that I couldn't feel my feet and stumbled but he held me in a warm embrace, as I knew he would do for the rest of my life.

CHAPTER 26

It took several very uncomfortable days for us to reach Carlisle from London.

I'd thought the snow would be worse in Scotland but the road was slippery but clear, as at long last, Godfrey drove a hired gig to take us to Gretna Green from our Inn at Carlisle.

I remembered the cold of our long journey north in the close confines of the coach, even with other passengers wrapped in cloaks and Tobias heavy on my lap. I pitied the people who sat, exposed, on the top of the coach with the armed guard – ready to defend the coach against highwaymen. Godfrey assured me that these ruffians were rare nowadays and that, anyway, he had his pistol to defend me.

I only wished we had more privacy to talk and even hold hands but that had to wait until we reached the different inns on the route, where we ate and slept while the horses were changed.

Despite the discomfort, I had found it very exciting to see new places. London's crowds had amazed me and later, I'd marvelled at the rolling hills and brief glimpses of frozen lakes. It was all jumbled in my mind, little villages and towns with tall church steeples and high buildings – all so different from the gentle Surrey countryside I knew so well. Godfrey pointed out places he knew and he held my hand, as if he realised the strangeness was almost overwhelming.

Now, in Scotland at last, he helped me down from the gig and insisted on carrying me down a narrow and muddy track to the forge where the Priest would wed us.

"I won't let you run away at the last moment, my love!" And he hugged me closer than was necessary. I had no intention of escaping but I did wish we were going to be married in a church, not by an unlettered man who called himself a Priest.

As I snuggled close to him, he said, "My darling Louisa – I thought you were so brave and uncomplaining on this long journey. Do you remember that time when the coach was stuck and we all had to get out and push?"

"Yes." I remembered it only too well. "It was a good thing you stopped that guard from attacking the gypsies who came to help us, thinking them robbers or highwaymen. We might still be pushing the coach if they hadn't come along! And the big fellow was so pleased when you gave him a shilling for his trouble. He said good fortune would follow us and we would have many handsome children."

I'd cherished those words, remembering the gypsy fortune-teller at the Fair. It was hard to believe it was barely three months ago – so much had happened in my life since then. I was still almost a child when I first met Godfrey but now I felt like a grown woman.

As my future husband carried me down the rough path, I thought back to the journey. We had spent several nights in different coaching inns, Godfrey insisting I had my own room. As I lay alone, with only Tobias to comfort me, I'd secretly wished Godfrey wasn't such a man of honour. Each night it had grown harder for us to part after such loving talk over supper but he had insisted, saying, "We have a life-time ahead of us, my darling."

Now, as he carried me over the rough and snow-covered ground, he said, "It's a good thing you are so light, my darling Louisa!"

I gloried in the warmth and safety of his arms.

The vast bulk of the blacksmith, Joseph Paisley, met us at the door of his cottage. He was almost as wide as he was tall, his jacket unable to meet over his huge chest.

"Come ye away inside, my dears," he boomed, blowing out great wafts of brandy. "As I told the Captain yesterday, I am the right Priest for you." His Scottish accent was so unfamiliar and thick I could hardly make out the words.

I doubted Mr. Paisley had ever been inside a church and again I longed for a proper clergyman, organ music, prayers and of course, to be wearing a beautiful silk wedding dress. I told myself off for such trivial thoughts. Marrying Godfrey was the only thing that mattered now.

As we came in, Mr. Paisley's toothless wife bobbed a curtsy.

We stood in front of a rough Cross, fashioned of bent metal, standing on an old anvil. Joseph Paisley opened a greasy-looking prayer book and mumbled the words at a great rate as we stood, hand in hand with Tobias sitting quietly beside us.

He slowed down for the final vows, Godfrey answering "I do," loudly but my heart was beating so fast my voice sounded breathless as I too answered, "I do."

Godfrey slipped the engraved gold ring he had brought onto my finger and Joseph Paisley said, "You be man and wife now." He leered at us. "You can kiss the bride, Sir."

We looked at each other and knew we would wait until we went outside this smelly cottage and away from the blacksmith's nasty stare.

I had a proper name at last – Louisa Macdonald, not that stupid Louisa La Coast which meant nothing.

"I shall save my kisses for later," Godfrey whispered to me. "Not in this place."

The papers were signed and witnessed by the Paisleys. The so-called Priest, Joseph, excited by the bag of money Godfrey gave him, asked us to drink brandy with him.

"No, thank you, Sir," Godfrey said. "My wife and I…" he said the words slowly, and with relish – "will go back to the

Inn for refreshment."

Outside, he held me close. "I shall love you for ever, *Till death us do part.* Our love will be like Shakespeare's sonnet on love and marriage you sent me – can you remind me of the words? At Oxford, I studied Latin, Greek and Mathematics, not poetry, alas, although you know I like it."

I remembered it well.

"Our love will be "an ever-fixed mark, that looks on tempests and is never shaken. It is the star..."

My words were lost as he gathered me up into his arms again, covering my mouth with kisses.